TRIBUTE

My mother's book.
Enjoy!

AG

Design by Sevy Perez
First Edition

ISBN: 978-0-9885873-4-2

Text set in Gotham HTF and Tisa OT
rescuepress.co

**RESCUE
PRESS**

TRIBUTE
ANNE GERMANACOS

MOM, FOR YOU

Should I ask the Professor if everybody folded
the rug on leaving, or if only I did this?

H.D., *Tribute to Freud*

If a novel tells a story whose true subject is time; if an essay is an attempt; if a notebook captures the quotidian. Doesn't Anne Germanacos's *Tribute* achieve all this? In her masterful second book, Germanacos gets right down to the elemental—the single line, fragment of scene or story or thought—and creates a book that may exist, inchoate, as all three of these forms: novel, essay, notebook, in continual shape-shift, exhilarating motion.

This restless relationship to form is born of that most elemental restlessness: desire. Germanacos documents desire's manifold incarnations, the body's and the mind's; she pays beautiful tribute to the force of desire and to those who have been bold enough to try to comprehend it (gentle echoes remind us of H.D. and her Freud). *Tribute* attests to its narrator's daily, embodied, erotic life—*Developing a voice with which to report back from the voiceless world of the body*? a central question and rightly eliding its subject—but also to her desire for and struggle against narrative. By moving only line by line, Germanacos shows how each sentence, or fragment thereof, is an impulse-toward, a trace left of desire. An impulse toward—narrative itself? You or I? The past, and those who may no longer hear us? These are the questions; I point you toward the wisdom that awaits you in *Tribute*.

The only way to tell a story is by taking time and slicing it, our narrator says, both acknowledging and mourning the task she takes on in her swift, agile strophes. She would like to render time, to offer story, with less violence and more freedom; her elusive form dares just this. As she leaps from line to line, she maps a great breadth of consciousness, exhibiting both rawness and rigor: she resists the conventions that would allow, or force, her to assume a more comfortable form. Novel, for instance, or memoir.

But let me contradict myself—an impulse Germanacos would understand. I do believe we can call *Tribute* a novel: it tells the story of a woman whose mother is dying, who begins to see an analyst, who lives among lovers and siblings and children and across continents and their conflicts. The novel offers us both her story—forcefully sensual, vibrantly lived—and, through this book's bold form, the complexity of her relationship to story.

Germanacos's language is straightforward, its observations the stuff of everyday life, but don't be fooled: her ambition is profound. *To go for the jugular*, our narrator wonders, as though idly, *just another way of talking about a harvest*? Throughout we feel how much this novel asked of the woman who made it. In correspondence Germanacos once said something to me of writing *whose form conveys the existential risk of its own making*, and this describes her *Tribute*: the narrator who comes to life within its pages puts herself at stake. Offers herself, perhaps, as tribute. For her endeavor—confession, trial, analysis, love song, dirge—is performed throughout with gratitude and love.

Writers like Germanacos remind us that to write *experimental prose* means playing with form, but this play can be an acute response to real need: a need to know the depths the old forms struggle to sound, the wildernesses they steer clear of. This approach is brave, not just for its skilled departures from convention, but for the risk at which it places the *I* we follow through these pages. In setting off into the hinterlands of novel, diary, essay, lyric, *Tribute* is in estimable company: in its explorations I imagine it encountering Clarice Lispector, David Markson, Marguerite Duras, Carole Maso, Maggie Nelson. These days that adjective *experimental* has gotten soggy, so much so we should probably just toss it. But if it means anything, it ought to mean the conjunction of courage and craft that we find in works like *Tribute*. It is an honor to publish this book, the first in an annual series of works of prose that, while diverse, we hope may all be this urgent and this exceptional.

Hilary Plum
Co-editor, Open Prose Series, Rescue Press
Spring 2014

TRIBUTE TO FREUD

I sit here typing

Thanksgiving got a little raucous. Afterwards, I went around picking up the pieces—but physical, not psychological.

•

My lips dried up completely.

•

Am I tired or is this just cold hands?

•

If she feels I've given up on her, will my mother die?

•

They swat her, making dust—skin, I guess—fly.

Monkeys, my sister says. We tend to snicker.

•

What, besides womanhood, do we have in common? Humanity?

•

Peeling the dead skin from my lips.

•

She said: Come on Thursday and we'll see if there's some way I can help you.

•

Can you eat canned pumpkin without cooking it?

•

(You're already talking.)

•

Fifty-one years into fifty minutes—an altered chronology.

•

This good Pinot leftover from Thanksgiving; tomorrow is December.

•

The fog beyond the window is brainy and alive.

•

Does it have to be cooked first?

•

My sister's limbs are smaller than mine, lanky, and fat-free.

When? We toss the question at each other—a swift, invisible Frisbee.

•

Sometimes my cycles (and compasses) get stuck on odd choices.

How to accompany her? How to land her home?

•

The therapist's office is above a liquor store; my husband is asleep in a distant time zone.

•

I asked the radiologist if the work gets tiring. It's fascinating, she said. No two persons' insides are the same.

•

Nervousness acts to disintegrate a sense of wholeness.

•

She said: When my time comes to die, remember me.

One fifty-minute session and I'm weeping in public.

•

A three o'clock appointment means that I'll keep her awake—or allow her to rest?

•

All her weakness is showing and she has no way of covering it up.

•

Now, there are (at least) two "she's".

•

Rain—relief.

•

Dream: I am eating body parts and realize that I've eaten a small piece of colon.

•

I know about clarity: greater clarity and lesser, and sometimes a clarity beyond what had previously seemed clear. And plenty of murk.

•

"Cocktail attire"? My closet is empty.

•

The sky was active, part of, not just backdrop to our conversation.

•

Nix on desire to go to the movies. Same re: invitations to holiday parties.

•

My friend said: It *is* cold, but if we were in New York, we'd think this was warm.

•

I may be able to get there—where I think I need to be—if I just keep going.

•

Trader Joe's—my eating club. Trader Joe's—my family?

•

In the black-and-white composition book the caretakers use to record her daily functions, I read that even on good days, my mother tells them she wants to die.

•

I kept saying that she is contained in me: digested and metabolized into psychic bone.

•

I asked if she was looking for bullet points.

•

Sometimes I remember them as they were—a long pause between breaths.

•

How are a wedding and a funeral alike? Often say one when meaning the other.

•

Sometimes I like to think I've left my mother in the dust—and then I don't.

•

As we spoke, the room went dark, mid-winter.

•

Your mind pops with the energy of newly released enzymes, synapses form, click.

•

She said, When you walk the dogs...

I said, I walk, but not with dogs.

•

A small Gumby stands on the low table beside her chair.

•

There's a slight sense of shame walking up those stairs.

•

I hardly remember what we said today but I know that I left happy.

•

Is laughter evil? What does Freud say about laughter?

•

I asked: What would the Freudians say about losing your notes twice?

She said: What would they say about losing them just once?

•

Pouring words and gestures into a fifty-minute hole.

•

(Good holes and bad.)

•

My feet are ice, my hands are thawing.

•

Rain gone. Cloud moving past the ceiling of blue sky.

•

She smiles, thank God.

•

She's right: I walked in scowling.

•

When you speak of "sickness," she said, you're not referring to anything mortal but something—

I'm talking about getting a cold.

•

One would like to be a yogi or a nun, seeking a single ray.

•

Trying to be gentle on my neck.

•

My friend thinks she got it by shaking hands with her mother's doctor.

•

My therapist has a bit of a British accent.

Does she?

•

Never give up the excitement located at the twisted core of a knot.

•

My mother was a mess until I handed her a rubber ball with blue sparkles inside it—she calmed like a baby with a pacifier.

•

She's inside a frame, behind a piece of glass.

Smudged?

•

Why wouldn't a person indulge in one or four dark-chocolate-covered whatevers?

•

There's that other thing, too. Small, but significant.

•

(Wills me into stillness.)

•

She thought I'd said oedipal pets.

•

The room darkened: she put her feet up underneath her, curled on top of them.

•

I know I seduce—attempt to seduce—

•

She snipped a tiny hole in my narcissistic binding.

•

Quips? Protect. (Hide?)

Feeling blasted through.

Diaspora daughter?

•

She said: I think it's something we don't have to attach a value to.

•

Penelope, waiting and teasing? Odysseus, tied to the mast?

•

Trickster? Or tricked?

•

Even when tricked, isn't there always another trick up the proverbial sleeve?

•

She said: Of COURSE it's hard.

•

Fishing for emotion.

•

Is this a fault, a quirk, or simply a habit?

•

My husband—flying to me as we speak.

•

At the party, the four of us sat in a corner, mumbling to each other in Greek.

•

If you're patient, the line can be a fine one. Impatient, the line may infuriate.

•

It was almost Christmas.

•

She escorts you there; she makes you say it.

•

In an erotic lull.

•

Or is it just that I'm eminently seducible?

•

The rain has stopped.

I can will calm and nimbleness.

•

Those bowls of bright candy.

•

We were speaking about fools.

She said, You look as if you're about to cry.

I said, I am crying, then wiped away my tears and smiled.

•

A three-alarm fire started nearby in the early hours of the morning; our emergency of desire was punctuated by passing sirens.

•

One could call it an expensive relationship—or one could simply call it rich.

•

She said: Oh, I don't know anything about other lives.

•

She called my definition reductive then drew attention to an array of possible uses.

•

Is she sending out tiny blatant messages to me?

•

She offered the perfect explication of a fool's place in the world.

•

Another parking ticket—oh well.

•

My mother fades and glows, fading, glowing. Inching along, inchworm, unmerrily.

•

Walking a windy avenue to the ocean, I take his hands and tell him: Here and here and here.

Then, I say: So now I'm wet.

•

I tell him that this voraciousness is entirely human.

•

Thinking that I'll be there in two hours, my stomach does a little thing.

•

Isn't candy always more promise than fulfillment?

•

Her rings tantalize and confuse.

•

Playful: her word, not mine, though I'm eager to adopt it.

•

Her eyes follow my hands as if they're intruders. To soothe her, I try to still them.

•

Without play, I am inept.

•

That pained silence.

•

Who laughs last—the therapist or the storyteller?

•

Does she stir troubles in her cup?

•

I have animal stories for you, I could say.

•

I am here, ready to be thrown off and if necessary, simply thrown.

•

My mother, like a reluctant kindergartner, requires being taken by the hand.

•

(I would like to throw her in the garbage can.)

•

Does she think it or dream it—a little of each?

•

Across the ocean, I often walk past piles of sheep shit—perfect round balls.

•

It was a hard day to be playful.

•

Excitement's sharp edge.

•

Like walking into the color created by sunlight through a ruby.

•

Life that refuses to sit still beside death, though they lie down together, and beautifully.

•

Watery would be one way of talking about it.

•

With so many objects—felt, imagined—who needs new furniture?

•

Sky lightening.

•

High buzzing in my stomach. Is that food or just nerves?

•

A streak of lightning, thunder-struck. Yellow sky.

•

Walking up the hill to the graves, my son asked: Are they cremated or full?

•

Some days, her decline is almost a kind of progress.

•

If only I could remember what we said: cut gems that flash color between our brains.

•

On that island, we lived next to a cemetery. Small memorial candles were visible to our sons from their room—a whole field of flickering lights, spooky or enchanting.

•

A laugh is a small seizure. As is, of course, an orgasm.

•

This may be an attempt at consummation.

•

Forgetting is fertile.

Let clarity take the long way around.

•

We talked about the importance of rituals—empty or not.

•

I've been to quite a few funerals but seem to miss the most important ones.

•

She said that it wasn't necessary to come many times a week.

Does she want me on a couch?

•

Once on the couch, does one never go back to sitting?

•

She from her vantage point and I from mine—but on the same horizon.

•

The door—also just a door.

•

It summoned, I surrendered, and then it deepened.

Confusion, murk add to the depth.

•

Last night we hardly slept.

•

Fooling around. Teasing?

•

He said: Just treat it as a fuck.

•

We're coming to the unwritten part.

•

Yesterday, I told her: I'm slightly terrified to say this but think I have to.

•

My sons and I speak her language almost fluently, understand it, generally, and tend to laugh at the absurdity of this comprehension.

•

This incessant movement between outer and inner, increasing sometimes to a frenzy.

•

I said: And seeing this as a legitimate way to have an affair.

She said: Oh, of course.

•

Revelation, or confession? Point of reference. Something to swim in together.

•

I give him everything.

•

It appears that I can be swept off my feet by all and sundry.

•

I'd like to talk about the necessary ubiquitousness of a mother.

•

Good-enough sex is not thrilling, but it can turn.

•

Voracious, though I would emphasize liveliness over greed.

There's something compelling about hunger.

•

Is it in anticipation that desire takes root? Vice versa?

•

Moving between life and writing—in all fairness, a kind of sex.

•

Has the world gone quiet or is it just me?

•

How calculated are a therapist's words?

•

I was simply saying that any architecture can be made holy by virtue of what goes on inside it.

•

She said: Oh, well, nothing is written in stone.

•

She said: People always talk to animals.

I said: But I talk "sheep" to the sheep, then baa'd for her.

•

I would say: it has hit with a vengeance.

•

She also said, Students are very compelling.

I could've said, So are teachers. And we might've laughed.

•

these waves that start small and sharp and open out to include—

Include? Collect.

•

I'll stay here, waiting.

This is what a patient must be: patient.

•

I sit here typing, my eyes closing every so often with the force of this thing.

•

I can be calm. I am fifty-one.

•

I sit here typing.

A quickly beating heart is the hint you have to take.

•

Does one need to do something with a state of arousal? Can't one simply live (in) it?

Do words drip?

•

That thing stuck up into the center—central within the central part.

Vortex, is the word I've been looking for.

•

The excitement of that possibility put me over the edge—or rather, on the edge, until I fell off, though possibly onto the wrong side.

•

To keep oneself vitally alive through writing? And then, in bliss and exhaustion, fall against a real human being with limbs, chest, lips, hands. Cock.

•

Creating the pages—the conversation in the mind   heightens the reality.

•

Saw a pretentious movie last night.

•

I can't help being a little obsessed with suitcases.

•

I told her that syllables of certain foreign languages are erotic, right at the place where sound and meaning overlap.

She seemed skeptical of my love for foreign languages—because they don't love you back?

•

General public knowledge of my mother's decline excuses me from undesirable social interactions.

•

The question is: Do I want another one of these pillows?

•

Called out to a squirrel this morning, but not in squirrel. I said hi as it scurried out from under a car.

Who do I think I am, telling her I speak to animals in their own tongue?

•

My fingers ache—taxed by all this necessity and desire.

•

The space between the incessant knots...

•

What are some of the things we were saying? Where are we now on the road to recovering what was apprehended?

•

Went to a crap movie last night. Didn't even finish my popcorn.

•

Adrift in uncertainty—bliss!

•

That friend said: That's all they ever want to talk about, anyway.

•

A compelling honesty. Or perhaps a *most* compelling honesty.

•

A treatise on sex? Sex and sunshine?

•

Sometimes, the only emotion is rage and all the pretty, beckoning lines—story lines, emotional lines, a little like the countless and unique wrinkles on a palm—go mute.

•

A long empty sleep on the beach may be reviving.

•

In a state of arousal, one hopes for some resolution.

And we're not necessarily speaking of orgasms.

•

Yesterday—gone—though the hope of its resuscitation hasn't died.

•

Writing—no, thinking—the words makes them come alive in the body.

•

The best part of so many movies is when you fall asleep—just for a second—and dream it from the inside.

•

Music rearranges tension, allowing it to find resolution—a form of repose.

•

An iPod inserted into the brain so you can live with a soundtrack, permanently enhancing your days?

•

You look at it, coolly, with immense warmth—and let it be.

•

The almost insupportable sadness of these days—trying to fix what's broken or partly damaged.

The beauty of the damaged parts.

•

Is writing cheating?

•

The brutality of living in a family—though I'm not willing to trade it.

•

Now, when I go to my mother's house in the afternoon, I toy with my iPhone, obscuring—stealing?—time. A minute of video for every day that's passed since Christmas.

•

I am a fiend for greens.

•

Back to Trader Joe's, back to life.

•

My hands are generally cold; my face hot. I use my face to warm my hands.

•

At one point, I found myself saying:

I wanted him, I got him.

•

She said something about desire and it bloomed.

•

How to sustain these things?

•

Aside from emotions attached to the transference, I believe she is kind.

•

Can one say, I desire desire?

•

I trust that she understood what I meant, whether she did or not.

•

Desire in the air.

•

It's a weather, entirely elemental but also connected inextricably to the brainstuff of us.

•

Always too much to sustain.

•

She said she wasn't disputing what I'd already let her know.

That, too, was a relief.

•

Hints like coded passwords encouraging me.

I said: It's become irresistible.

•

The habit of chocolate is stultifying.

•

Fury. This is what it tastes like.

•

Beyond imagining any surprises right now.

•

As always, one writes toward the possibility of ecstasy.

•

Today, she wore a skirt and black stockings that showed off her calves.

•

Clean mammograms, clean endometrial biopsy.

•

All of us attempting to fuck our way through life?

•

Stop being so picky and let yourself dissolve.

•

A little stunned. If this is the way it's going to be, I think I can take it.

•

Aren't names—and what one feels comfortable calling another person—strange?

•

When the sun sets, it is sometimes so odd to look back and try to trace the way you've been in the world.

•

I am falling off,

•

Speaking of the child acting that part, she said he was "delicious."

•

Desire can fuel you through the day; it has to fuel you through a life.

•

She said: It could be absolutely infuriating for the reader or the reader could get lost in the fantasy.

•

She said: You play with accusation in relation to that incident.

I said: I wouldn't want to take sides.

•

In comparison to the beserker bears, she said, fairy tales are more like lullabies.

•

That word: beserk.

•

Light came in through the southern window. I felt bathed by it, though she might have thought I was stewing.

•

It's harder to say things aloud.

•

What's done is done.

•

Does she have breast cancer? Or was she reading those pages to prepare for a class?

•

No matter how passive and uninvolved a mother may be, she'll still be construed as controlling. She said it, not I.

•

I would like to feel I've left her with a better impression—my perception of her impression keeps darting back at me.

•

Like looking out and seeing everything covered in snow—and not being able to appreciate the beauty of white, glare, and silence.

•

Time is in flux—unusual, elongated, shortened.

How to weather it?

•

Do you get your (lost) self *back* or do you get back *to* it?

•

If I were to give up candy, would a safe return be guaranteed?

•

Or is sorrow something that needed to happen?

•

And then I panicked that I wouldn't be able to sustain a belief in my fate.

•

Slayed.

•

Haven't had a moment's rest.

•

I would like to ask her: What is your opinion on the adult consumption of candy?

•

It is good to bring down a suitcase from the attic, good to bring up empty boxes from the basement.

•

If you can't make something decent out of interruptions, you're doomed.

•

What's the difference between a panic attack and existential terror?

•

His hands, approaching, force sound from me.

•

This, here, is my home.

•

Go back and reexamine (fear).

•

Hubris?

•

It is easy to buy expensive wine and pleasant to imbibe it.

•

The sadness that holds these two parts together.

•

There is no going back.

•

Reading about the first cemeteries in San Francisco, dating back to the 1860s.

•

Got stuck in an expectation of desire's fulfillment—

•

How to turn terror to exuberance? Wordless lullabies.

•

That long strand of purple beads gives the patient something to focus on, something you want to touch.

•

My mother has three rubber balls with glitter and water inside. One has a red strobe that lights up when you bounce it. Bounce, a word she no longer understands.

•

An erotic inquiry? An inquiry into eros? A bit of porn, a smidgen of philosophy.

•

He misses his animals and trees, his rocks, and weather that allows him to shout at it. Who can blame him? *Ellada* has its beauties.

•

Some sessions, I'm mute, bursting with conversation but unable to utter a word.

•

Sadness offers repose.

•

When I lost myself first to fear then to sadness, I also lost the pain in my neck.

•

The world does sit out there, not exactly waiting.

•

It's about that gaze—which can be imagined in the best of times, is otherwise longed for.

•

Times when everything is incredibly sexy.

•

My muted cruelty toward him seemed to come back at me

tenfold. That night, I had to relearn the very old trick of rocking myself to sleep.

•

It was her eyes on me as I wrote the words, imagining the act committed in the pulse of them.

•

Hungry, or about to turn hungry.

•

The anticipation of candy increases the reverie; putting it in one's mouth does nothing to improve the dream.

•

Wine may deepen it.

•

When she said: Sometimes when we feel tightly wound, it's because we feel squeezed.

I could've asked: Where does a squeeze begin?

When she said: Maybe you feel I expect something from you.

I might have said: I want this to be a good conversation.

•

My biceps are uneven; I can't help it.

•

There is a whole quantity of dream life butting up against the words; it forces an entrance.

•

Funny the way I've put a circle around this thing.

•

There are many erotic loves, not all of them specifically sexual.

•

I guess I have to go set the table, make the salad.

•

Gumby's maker died.

Tropical fish dying in Florida.

Heavy snow and unusual cold in northern Europe.

Race riots in southern Italy.

•

Playing iPhone skeeball while talking with my mother, I wonder if I will forget her face and think of a narrow lane, balls flung toward virtual holes when—down the road—I hear her voice in my head, if I do.

•

Hungry for an appreciative audience.

•

A watershed?

•

Things to discuss: this, that, and that. I guess that's all I'm willing to say.

•

He interrupted me—to an extent—by guessing who it was for. But, at the same time, we'd just kissed with something that— if not abandon—was extremely close.

•

Bursting with gifts for her.

•

Miep Gies, the woman who helped hide Anne Frank, died today at 100.

•

I like it when my mind is silenced by the touch our bodies make.

Silenced, or quieted, at the very least.

•

I told her: We had an interesting encounter last night. She said: I take it you mean a sexual encounter.

This, after our dalliance with glances.

•

I haven't told her the story about the raccoon.

•

you lower your gaze, but only until desire drives you back again

•

All I know is that since then, it has both increased and I've been more outspoken about it.

•

This is a token of his debt to you, I said. Then added: A token of his gratitude to you through me.

•

While he slept, I lay awake for a long time, thinking his body onto mine. The merest fluttering of fingertips.

•

Not many thoughts today—all swallowed up.

•

I keep thinking about Freud's genius.

•

The conversation won't end; there's hardly a pause.

•

She reached out once I'd turned away and touched my right shoulder. And then I was out the door.

•

There were several times when I wanted to say: Stop talking and look at me, please. Or simply: Stop talking!

•

There is a kind of Aphrodite of Paphos in glass and a bear-looking thing in what may be white marble. Why can't I remember these things? I only remember Gumby.

•

What to do with this? Create a paean to Freud? A piece of pornography?

•

She said: Oh, we're way beyond that point!

•

Putting something good in my mouth does it, too.

•

Speaking of writing, she said, Freud wrote every day.

•

Sometimes I don't quite understand what she says; sometimes words don't exactly matter.

•

Whatever is in me rushes out to meet him. I can't stop it or myself—whichever is which.

He's leaving in an hour.

•

We'd like it if some things would go on forever.

•

In the counter-transference, does the therapist feel what the patient feels?

Or do her slowly closing eyes (animal-like, cat-like) merely mimic mine?

•

Somewhat deliciously out of control

He told me to be careful.

•

Sick with it

•

Fingers, tongues, in everything resembling a hole, any indentation or curve.

•

If she's not feeling some small portion of what I'm feeling

•

He is flying away this minute.

•

How to translate it?

•

this sexual sea

•

I think I can do this.

•

Because I move quickly between the modes—real and imagined—I can keep generating the psychological circumstances that will allow me to keep it alive?

•

In trying to hold on, I will only lose (hold).

•

Developing a voice with which to report back from the voiceless world of the body?

•

We haven't said a word denoting color—or have we?

My husband is almost in Europe.

Is this settling into normalcy?

•

I could ask: Have you seen the Aristocrats?

•

Moments of repose arrive thick with it.

Do we really get to keep doing this? Really?

•

The kind of weather I can't resist.

•

Have I seen anything? Anything interesting with my eyes? This landscape is entirely internal.

•

Pleasure is always mixed with pain?

•

Swallowing, I think of him.

•

This insistence on stillness, a stillness within which the body will begin to move—and not stop until it has worn itself out against the flesh of another.

•

I have to eat dinner. It's almost ten o'clock.

•

He said: Don't do anything rash.

•

I will shower her with—petals? Snowflakes?

•

The thing flooded in, again.

•

I made sure to say that the opposite of authentic in this case was not "fake."

•

Having my cake with her, eating it with him?

•

This morning I leaned over the newspaper, reading, and let out a small moan.

World events?

•

Feeling quakes into me as my mother slowly dies.

Death, also a climax.

•

In that room, I have said "turned on." I have said "have sex." I have said "a sexual indiscretion" and also "an interesting encounter."

She said: I take it you mean a sexual encounter.

•

Coming, I could say, is not a problem.

•

Orgasms may seem like a travesty—or simply beside the point.

•

Martin Luther King's birthday. Rain.

•

Crying to sadness is like sex to desire. Sometimes you prefer the diffuseness of emotion rather than its release.

•

And then he drew images on the palm of my hand, all of us in the small cabin of a truck, five of us, I think—and the two of us in a world, swirling.

We fucked on a rock, while the others ate bread and feta cheese down below on the beach.

•

This relationship is not out in the world, but it's in the world.

We sit opposite and I open, and open again.

•

It takes some words, a glance toward her—a pause—then a swoop upward to find her gaze on mine: steady, waiting, cat-sleek.

•

I am beating up my hands, shoulders, neck with the intensity of this need.

The wear and tear of it.

•

Writing's climax tends to be in the brain. You could say it's an abuse of the (poor) body.

•

Food on its way to the stomach becomes confused—or entangled with—sexual arousal.

•

Back to the beginning of life, when mother and child went from one to two, in order to be able, soon now, to be one without her.

•

I am trying to put things down in order both to free and form them.

•

The death of a parent allows the (grown) child to be reborn, slightly otherwise.

•

Mouth, container of words and saliva, hope chest, taste.

•

Stomach—all parts are involved in the stifling or conniving of what surrounds it. Nervous pangs like misdirected sexual charges...

•

Just one thing about paranoia: Lop it out, or it'll stick and cavort with everything dark.

•

A time whose fecundity cannot last forever.

•

Some glass fragment lodged here: the thought of losing him.

•

The sun is out. Blue sky above, cloud to the west.

•

The importance of being fluent in a form.

•

Or just a blasted confusion?

•

My mother wore a black-and-white wool scarf with a small mint-green stain—her ice cream. I told her she looked like a Palestinian and she answered that she wants lots of men around her.

An Arafat?

•

In funeral parlor language, HOP stands for Home of Peace.

•

My mother says: I want to die. And then she says: But I love you!

•

Is this my last chance to get my story down? (Am I treating it as if it were?)

•

My husband has arrived in a mostly cold place.

•

My mother sits in her chair, all too aware of her desires: she wants to be like us.

•

That woman, too, is a kind of mother. She frees me to avoid my own—even if just for an hour.

•

There are now several iterations of that event.

•

I simply allow it to bring us—to take us—to offer us—

Sometimes still retreating in a panic of guilt and anxiety.

•

It was and still is easy to give that flight-long headache as the reason—but that's not what I went there to talk about.

•

I stared at her or toward her and was taken by my own capacity for the erotic. It's not that it had exactly evaded me, but when it seemed to desert, I missed it profoundly.

•

She brought the possibility of sex—in every sphere, dot, line, and plane—to fruition.

•

For the moment, the rain has stopped.

•

Some days, I go from the real-but-artificial erotic gaze straight to the original.

Boundaries fall away: mother of my mother, and she, child of her child.

I don't mean to exploit a painful situation, but there's bliss in it, too.

•

Having found the larger story, I have also found the solution to the problem.

•

What colors in her mind, what news in her heart?

•

I keep refusing to give my friends and acquaintances the time of day.

•

She always says: Oh, I haven't read the paper yet.

•

The room, of course, is a kind of body.

•

A lively, occurring present—you snap to attention and keep snapping.

•

Some days, sex sits high in the stomach, nervous of its descent.

The mind's job? Urge it downward, lighting every place along the way.

•

Thick blue-grey and pink clouds to the west.

•

When I asked, Who am I? She said: You're you!

•

My hands feel this pressing need to act, think, and make—all at once and constantly.

•

Maybe, together with me, he will be in awe of a small thing.

Though again, perhaps not.

•

After all, it's the talking cure!

•

Cloudy with blue skies and sun. 8:15 a.m. I am pale—winter-struck.

•

My eyeballs are hot.

The rainbow is gone. So is the blue sky.

•

I walk into that room, full of what I want to say, and empty of it, too, holding everything back so that anything new might take its place.

•

How will I manufacture an excuse as good as my mother?

•

Background events: the earthquake in Haiti.

•

Rain.

•

Pouring.

•

Experience comes different when spoken.

•

Freezing.

•

World-fuck?

•

Some blossoming—gathered.

•

She garbles words, confuses intention, can't follow a simple line of narrative—but still gets the gist.

•

I keep leaving trails of words, like candy or crumbs.

•

So I have made of her—what? Or who?

And my stepfather's grave.

•

There's so much more to it than what we sometimes allow it to be.

•

I would like to spread my body against his.

•

Time for a walk.

•

That other story, an addendum.

•

He left, then she left. My body hasn't stopped hurting.

•

I like the idea of talking with people; I like knowing that I'll be alone.

•

Pain makes you notice your body when you've been ignoring it?

•

Sometimes, in the middle of the night

•

Are these spooky times or is this just the beginning of a cold?

•

A capitulation like an emptying out.

•

From H.D.'s *Tribute to Freud*: "I wanted to know at what exact moment, and in what manner, there came that flash of inspiration, that thing that clicked, that sounded, that shouted in the inner Freud mind, heart, or soul, *this is it*."

•

Just boiled greens, and in a separate pot leeks, mushrooms, and baby bok choy.

•

Two tongues: the one that speaks, the other that writes slowly on the body.

•

Fluffy clouds against blue sky.

•

The camera allows me to see her more clearly, saves me from complicated emotions.

•

Taking her into my body in order to keep and have her.

•

I have nothing against stealing time; that it's impossible doesn't keep me from trying.

•

Draw the line?

Erase?

Thinking of that last night with him makes my eyes burn.

•

Tossed around by a force.

•

Take into consideration all holes, every part.

•

I suppose it's like acting—

•

More than hints of pink. Defined areas of pink. And thick, endless cloud to the west. Grey, blue. Morning.

•

Getting closer to death has its rewards.

•

I am a little at large.

•

About to draw the curtain on this scene.

•

Packing. Spinning a little out

•

A haunting and a grieving but also a stage.

•

If there's no possibility of being fucked by it

•

She spoke, allowing me simply to nod.

Unable to look at her.

•

The plum tree is filling out with pink blossoms.

•

I said: It's always been a form of seduction for me.

•

I could hear my breath as I waited for the words to coalesce.

•

Toward the end she said: Your dream didn't come true.
And I said: True.

•

She said: Did you think this was conditional?

•

Choosing appropriate erotic offerings.

•

Sometimes the motion of offering words turns into a kiss.

•

Leafing through porn, sex manuals.

•

She said, Oh, you know those Imagists. What can you make of a tissue box?

•

The mouth stops being the outlet for words and dissolves, then every thought ends in the body.

•

The bubble has popped.

Which one, she asked.

All of them.

•

All that arousal for nought; it quickly leaked away.

•

And who do you think you are, going around in those skintight yoga pants?

•

Unable to right myself. Barely here.

She wanted to know what happens during separations. This is an accurate enough picture.

•

Cure what, exactly?

Looking out on the brown and darker-brown park.

•

Cross-Atlantic pillow talk.

•

Would it be inappropriate to say: Thinking of him takes my breath away.

•

Sunlight on the buildings at the edge of the park.

•

Those times growing up when—a woman's body, her hands or face reminded me of my mother and I sort of swooned in longing or maybe despair.

•

Light gone. Bright orange reflected off two windows to the west.

The word "west" produces an ache.

•

This part of the story continues: New York.

•

Incendiary!

•

To bed, I suppose.

•

She had the most washed-free-of-everything-but-sadness eyes I'd ever seen. I already knew, but asked anyway. "Haiti," she said, giving me her eyes.

•

Does caffeine cut down erotic feeling?

•

Moving between tears and the physical manifestations of the erotic.

•

Even in moments of nervousness or panic, one can find a route to calm by listening to the body.

•

Off to the Met.

•

Woke up to a vision of white—and nothing beyond the faint outlines of the buildings on the north side of the block.

•

This sore throat seems to have become a habit.

•

How to celebrate the body? (How to render it celebratory?)

•

Is this something I was supposed to have learned at the beginning?

•

This, a self's civil war.

•

Grey, a favorite color?

•

When the body begins to hurt, it's easy to punish it for the mind's mistakes. You panic at the impasse.

•

Note what happened on that long plane flight: essentially, war between the states.

•

This bluing city with tall dark buildings. Lights coming on.

•

A bottom-of-the-barrel kind of sex—alone, of course, and of necessity a little desperate, a little doomed.

•

Snow forces isolation. Up in a tower, alone.

Rapunzel?

Some fairy tale I'm not familiar with?

•

Going out into the blizzard.

•

The future seems

My head is off; my mind, too.

•

Where do people learn to talk in such a precise, ziplocked way?

•

Snow on the ground.

•

Sometimes you feel that everything you've done marks you as inferior. Sometimes it changes.

At some point, we give up religious stories for stories of justice.

But are we capable of being rational?

•

Wanting to knit. Missing knitting out of the blue.

•

Cleaning graves?

•

Do wounds accumulate?

•

Embarrassed by former selves

•

Her inability to let herself off the hook.

•

Cure?

•

Happy ending?

•

When is a relationship "over"?

•

How does anything "end"?

•

Phillips: "An analysis is never finished, it is only abandoned."

•

Mesmer: a seducer and a fraud

•

How to tell a story? Up for grabs? Under debate.

•

One day last month, my mother expressed an interest in candy.

•

Thinking about stories—chronologically inept, emotionally fraught.

•

Audience?

•

And then I came to (erotic) attention.

•

The mental terrain of the western world rolled up on that particular shore.

•

Animated by humble desire.

•

This, and my mother, too.

•

Ride this wave
(then we'll see)

•

Choose the right stick of dynamite.

•

I arrived ready to surrender.

•

Eating is now a question of hunger, not appetite.

•

My husband's playful rocky landscape, his animals, our sheep.

•

You would never take a list; the hour must begin with a new syllable.

•

Not saying the things would be cowardly; at the same time, you need to walk in empty.

•

There must be a difference between burying a mother and burying a father.

•

Jealous that H.D. knew Freud?

•

Is that rain?

•

My breathing would've gone odd.

•

The real crunch of snow outside the 72nd St. train station.

•

Spoke with a Liberian taxi driver.

•

Met a congressman.

•

Starving, despite all those peanuts.

•

Accustomed to coming; being endlessly responsive is something else.

•

The way mind sometimes folds into the body.

It has started again.

•

Recognized the widow of a famous man.

•

I keep saying: unravel. But don't I mean disentangle?

•

She said: Mom is floridly psychotic.

•

(Perfect) concentration, (perfect) self-forgetting.

•

Home.

Prolonging the moment of entrance, the moment we ache for.

•

How to court surrender?

•

There is wind; raki goes straight to the body.

•

Psychological pitfalls. Downfalls? Is there a difference?

•

The snow came down, alternating with a swirl. At first, everything was darkened by the white.

I am home.

•

Our life here may be thin, but it's very rich.

•

He says he has a sliver, and wants to bathe the hand in something antiseptic, first.

•

We have not stayed together all these years merely because

•

A woman's sexuality goes through her mother.

•

My husband has to fight me off.

•

Like a mother, but not. She watches me all day long, or not.

•

This text plays through me; this text won't let me eat.

•

I guess this is the story I've been writing.

•

The points on the line where we happen to be augment this always-present-but-sometimes-quiet sexual feeling?

•

No two people rise and fall at the exact same rate, despite the importance placed on mutual orgasm—in a slightly different, but overlapping sphere.

•

Not yet twenty-four hours here and the story continues, finds its way, water flows.

•

And one more thing: I am open to hearing voices, but I would
never call them God.

•

Anything can set it off

•

But on the third night, he turned away from my cold hands and I
was bereft.

•

You and your mortality-induced heat!

•

Milking my mother's presence in the world for all it's worth:
When she's gone, the only milk will be my own.

•

A mouth, involved or invoked—and how it increases the yield of
the exchange.

•

Figs and my husband's mutton soup for breakfast.

•

No doubt sex is a form of eating and being eaten.

•

If some sliver of eternity enters lovemaking then, also, at least a
grain of death enters as well.

The grain may push us to a moment's oblivion, or stop us in our
tracks.

•

Are there deeper reasons than sex and curiosity?

•

That road turned slightly sour.

•

Perhaps this is an impossible task; we're all made of legion selves.

•

Some form of you, not you at all but me—but me with *you* inside

•

What kind of bras are these?

•

The sexiness of money, (the currency of sex).

•

My mother has no conception of distance. All of it—temporal, spatial—is huge and terrifying.

•

No pressure to speak with anyone at all, but him.

•

Sometimes it stops; sometimes it's stopped up.

•

Awfully taken with myself—my body and its ways.

•

Perhaps it's not pleasant to read someone else's version of it.

An affront? An aggression?

•

Intense, fragile beauty can be created along the interstices of a life.

•

In another sense, though, isn't my whole adult life a case of being swept away?

•

Waxing crescent.

•

What does it mean to be ravished?

•

When he is under the weather, I generally feel as if I've got something to do with it.

•

There is good sex and there is enough sex—and the two can't always overlap.

•

I don't like that story, though I know I'll tackle it—eventually.

•

In other words: some things that need to be said, outright. Some things that one finds one's way to saying.

•

What is it that writing does to a life?

•

There, she becomes a kind of page—no more blank than any other.

•

Isn't every page written over with thousands of illegible words?

Love insists: Put new words there with the old ones.

•

She, too, is a person.

•

Was it reasonable for me that day to simply look, wanting something I couldn't have?

•

Waiting for him to replenish.

•

Time for a shot of tsikoudia.

•

Our days are long, our days are profitable.

•

My mother says they're beating her up and that if I like her—she asked, "Do you like me?"—I'd better get back there soon.

The salient feature of my life?

Or mere alibi?

•

Outside, they are hacking branches off trees—my idea of a good time, not his.

•

I folded myself into him, awakening him. What time is it, he asked, and then, let's sleep. I stayed up longer, crying a little, undone that I'm so undone.

•

In the right mood this place is a paradise: sun, sea, birds, light. Earth, olive trees, anemones.

•

I'm not sure I'm saying this correctly: the satisfaction of physical hunger is registered sexually. That may be what I'm trying to say.

•

I shouldn't be identifying with the schizoids he describes in that book.

•

Walked to the iconostasis and back.

•

She said, How do you feel about that—being a patient?

I said: I can be patient.

•

Facing the page, it turns out, is a lot like facing the sun of your therapist's face.

•

Next time I'm in that room, I would like to say: Did you feel it—at least a tiny bit? Like a shadow or a cloud, a light rain or a subtle change in the air's scent?

•

Less problem than task, but one that embraces you as you close your arms around it.

•

I watched him from above while he tossed something—fertilizer?—at the base of his trees, then stood there, looking at them. As he walked away, his gaze crossed mine. He laughed and said that he knew someone was watching him, but he'd thought it was God.

•

To be stabbed in your innermost body by hunger for another's touch?

•

I'm having trouble being violent with time; in the past, I've chopped it up mercilessly.

•

Things that are good for therapy may not be good for stories, and vice versa.

But I don't believe it.

•

One creates steel when it's required.

•

Morning, a lively time.

•

You always leave the water running just a little—to prevent the pipes from freezing.

•

Hands always—if we're to be perfectly frank—on one set of keys or another.

•

Those chairs and the way they allow each of us to seat ourselves—in relation to the cup of the chair, of course, but also in relation to each other.

We zig and zag, two grown women engaged in lively conversation with some dash of seduction thrown in.

•

Sometimes I lean down to straighten the rug—like a body of water, connecting us, two islands. Other times, that rug an island and we, the sea surrounding.

•

Is it the fact that I've done quite a few moon salutations tonight?

•

Moderating terror. Mediating terror?

•

A rush of closeness. A seal on us?

•

Most days, aside from my husband, they're the only people I see: father and teenaged son, their thick-muscled arms squeezing milk from warm flesh into a silver pail at their feet. On quiet days, I can hear the milk hitting the tin.

A young man with ropy forearms squeezes the flesh of a ewe years before tracing circles on a young woman's nipples with a fingertip.

•

Each sentence, a thrust?

•

And then things came clear.

•

That earthworm muscled along: first the front, then the back, an undulation.

•

Circumstances seemed to come together in such a way that

•

This thing could hang over me for hours, I think.

•

I'm not sure that he's up to it; I have to be.

•

It depends on what you think you want, in the end: story or sensation. But maybe one doesn't preclude the other.

•

No neat endings.

•

The sheep are starting to lamb. Two black ones, confused, began to follow me up the hill.

I, a ewe.

•

There's always that question of killing or almost killing, mostly an effort to claim self-sufficiency in the firm knowledge of uncertainty.

•

But what are you suggesting?

•

It's all tied up with the certainty of uncertainty: the body, ever open to suggestion.

POLITICS

rejoicing, in my own quiet but occasionally sole-slapping way

•

maintaining tension, modulating it

•

full moon—mooning around

•

Holding onto a secret has its price: you pay until you can't.

•

Like a good analyst, like a good mother, a story holds.

•

(a sliver of perfection)

•

Some organizing part of me goes dumb.

•

no ledge, no circle of earth, no leg

•

Shaping, you kill.

•

some half-assed Michelangelo, chipping away

•

bliss?

•

one line for me, and another line for me

•

(within her sight)

•

suffer deprivation patiently?

•

How about saying OM and calling it a day?

•

reveal how revelation occurs?

•

these spasms of sex—a little like sobs

•

just one long, familiar book with gods and goddesses

•

fiction, right?

•

fragment by fragment

•

around and around and down various paths
having taken myself down to the nails

•

either way, divided

•

preparing to believe

•

(a lifetime of no's)

•

a second of immortality

•

I'm supposed to listen to my mother flail around in outer space, then put down the phone and eat my dinner?

•

feels like homicide (better than suicide)

•

these words: a kiss you can't refuse

•

no guarantee?

•

simply to stare at the blank page—which is, as I've said—a version of her face

•

(splaying myself, being splayed)

•

Who decides an alter ego? You do, no doubt.

•

Shouldn't I be reading?

•

very sort of happy, cheerful, lively, and light-hearted

•

There's the problem of desire, and when that's not a problem, there's the other one.

•

I turned

•

Corners open out, edges turn in. Opposites dissolve in a unity that contains everything, including small sexual indiscretions.

•

the absolute luck of that occurrence

•

no regrets, no turning back

•

Begin here?

•

How to say anything at all without suggesting the body's acute silence?

•

sort of myself, sort of not

•

Religion and sand go in the same box.

•

(sometimes inhabited by a god)

•

Fleet things do occur.

•

a swift presence in the quick-burning oxygen of a brain—

•

thought "I love you" without knowing

•

always dreaming hard

•

call it tears

•

licked his shin

•

You go in with the light and come out into the dark.

•

accidental connections, artistic reveries

•

messy

•

not much of a self to sell or fight for

•

Clouds may look distinct.

•

(merge in the blink of an eye)

•

a neatly tied-up package

•

eminently penetrable

•

Sex sews up the borders?

•

Today, in some version of a hangover, my body hurts.

•

The new cats run down the vertical of that rock, slip away into the green.

•

omnipotence, grandiosity, exhibitionism

•

Tapped, you thrum.

•

The sky splits open—memories rain.

•

I picture myself arriving, a little panting, a little dog.

•

(yesterday, on that bed)

•

not sure about strength; familiar with the obstinacy of weakness

•

Tender, delicate, intricate: one may crave a violent rupture.

•

(real? *really* real?)

•

That picture is untouched, but I was wearing makeup, of course.

•

New York in the snow?

•

What would be the opposite of punishment?

•

(What would be the next opposite?)

•

need to take my vitamins

•

inching along

•

A bad wife and a bad person? A bad wife but an exciting person?
An exciting person precisely because a bad wife?

•

Slay me, I'm bad.

•

(sixth day of a headache)

•

the opposite of magic? *bad* magic

•

but a stunning headache: bright, with brilliant glints!

•

Pain humbles me; I embrace him.

•

(my body, my window)

•

a doorman, a little like a woman, with her lintels and buttons and
locks

•

my nerves, centrally located, so to speak

•

bypassing mind

•

slip out the back door

•

hens and roosters against the buttercups—spring

•

dark-haired carcass of a goat caught on a wire

•

small bits of something white glistening in the mid-afternoon sun

•

(pear)

•

not getting anywhere, are we?

•

when to capitulate, when to recede?

•

meat and greens for lunch, dinner, and breakfast

•

Our mother drools, my sister tells me in an email from another planet.

•

Do you go under willingly or with a fight and which of the two yields more?

•

flush with who I am

•

I do love this underwear, lace like a cloud.

•

always open to discussion: how much of it you'd really want to see in reality

•

So how did that happen?

•

And I love him.

•

a lizard turning somersaults

•

orange butterfly, dead goat

•

It switches quickly and the back of my neck begins to talk.

•

food, sometimes an interruption

•

Time squeezes more than any person or situation.

•

the children? a little vague these days, back-burnered

•

stupid, or just cowardly?

•

"Appetite will be a good story for you if you are lucky enough to have the right mother." (Phillips)

•

Is there a problem or am I just trying to stir things up?

•

How many unread books...

•

Important sins, he said, laughing, and turned away.

•

that dead goat—not talisman but reference

•

I kill him with thoughts?

•

bashing up against the ramparts of me

•

right here, now: sun coming in from the west

•

desired?

•

(just a finger)

•

an adjustment between thinking it and doing it

•

as close to miraculous as anything, ever

•

I also need to talk about my husband's body, his mouth.

•

Is that the crack you're trying to walk?

•

throw suggestion at him like a blunt object

•

the beginning of your political life?

•

even if, at this juncture, you want him incessantly

•

How to waltz this divide?

•

go back there carrying this thing in my hands?

•

(nothing to do with packing bags)

•

I sit by the fire, watching his face, watching the skin on his bones

•

sleep now, please?

•

the world—a little oystery these days

•

doing the things men and women do

•

childish depths?

•

zigzag to mitigate the angle of the descent

•

(adult heights)

•

Something is a little missing.

•

I need a bag, a conduit, a ribbon, a line in the sand. A rubber band, a cup, your mug, a dollar.

•

what I've got? broken eggshells, crusty with bits

•

arriving at the surface, look closely and take notes

•

out of the blue, Chicago

•

barely seeing

•

Double click to open a file? Certain things open me, as well—one click.

•

He wants tender kisses; mine are greedy and sexual.

•

This whole contraption down there stands on its hind legs, begging.

•

A story, in addition to being a transference, is the resolution of one.

•

Imposter is the word I was looking for.

•

(shoulders squared)

•

that array of grilled things: peppers in four colors, mushrooms, and salty haloumi

•

Feeling hostile toward my sister does nothing good for my sex life.

•

(cupcakes that looked delicious but weren't)

•

bright spring day; an overflow of yellow

•

working my way through the emotions

•

(they arrive in pairs)

•

A symbol on the keyboard saved me!

•

expansive days, contracted days

•

in the market for a little ecstasy

•

a parallel life on a bed, a raft, a table, or against a wall

•

Years ago, I wanted to jump and didn't, then did. This is different.

•

on the lookout for augurs: staring at the sky, startled by birds

•

that huge plain of everything beyond

•

(inklings)

•

Stretch this thing taut—its plucking will ring true.

•

an awareness of the mechanics of the machine, how it runs, what makes it stop and go

•

constantly chatting her up—this her in me

•

blasted through or about to be

•

limping, crying

•

astonished

•

trying to be open-minded, trying to be confident

•

What's the difference between a spasm and a contraction?

•

(Does a body ping more or a brain?)

•

I spoke with my mother yesterday—it was like speaking with someone who couldn't.

•

She's right: I set up the transference as soon as I have a hint of its possibility.

•

Small birds often fly into the glass of our windows making a plonk that startles me and knocks them out, but only for seconds.

●

a keen intensity—a *most* keen intensity

●

from one minute to the next and I have no idea what makes it happen

●

antioxidants?

●

just us and us, with some books thrown in

●

He says he cut into his finger as if it were the bread he was trying to slice.

●

He's taking the fish off its bones; I'm biting my cheeks raw.

●

The smell of food cooking may also register in that way.

●

Amazing how quickly some words, put together, want to call themselves a story.

●

Contiguous, friction occurs.

●

Keep at this thing that keeps yielding?

●

I could put it under a microscope;
I could examine two things side by side.

•

A finger is just a finger.

•

dreamt a small doll moving across the floor

•

Like a tree, but the kind of tree that can open its legs.

•

sadness, a (soft) boulder

•

Looking at my face reminds me of my skull.

•

Black cat (dabs of white on each paw) licks a puddle.

•

In profile, goats are always smiling.

•

always rising from the dirt

•

shudder—a word I read in a story

•

(clench)

•

progress?

•

(like a hawk)

At first, I couldn't say a word, as if she's a mind-reader, which she both is and isn't.

•

a patient, so open to suggestion

•

rain in the night

•

How can you stand this flood of inarticulate talk?

•

almost all of it happening in the patient's mind

•

The plum tree, just beginning to bud in early February, is thick now with dark red leaves.

•

(Last night, Jews flicked drops of wine like so many plagues.)

•

My mother asks me if I have children, then wonders where her daughter is.

•

A fat yellowjacket bumps against the window.

sun from the east, one thick cloud
rising gull, gentle wind

•

lost my knack?

•

sun and rain, interspersed

•

It may not be real but it *feels* as if it is.

•

one dip

•

(two)

•

writing—aggressive by nature

•

I think it up, she lets it happen?

•

That friend called it a masterfully convincing bit of (shaped, controlled) diary.

•

because I allowed myself to construe it as gift

•

Glancing away, you break the lock, the seal, the spell.

•

photographers?

•

I said: But sex comes from all different places.

She said: Of course it does.

•

handed me a

•

You, I said.

•

Patient may be precisely what I'm not.

•

the plum tree—so thick with leaves, shimmery and wild

•

examined through a lens

•

not envious of mothers with babies or even conductors with their orchestras

•

She said: It was just to see each other again.

•

One day I may need to ask: How old are you, anyway?

•

carrying the world in a (portable) word

•

my children when they were small

•

weeping in the snow

•

this pimple

•

nostalgic for a different kind of narrative?

•

I said: Right now, they're hammering Jesus to the Cross.

•

(Aren't the words bier and pyre almost the same?)

•

I watched them speak, embrace, pull apart. She stepped back into the doorway of her building.

•

feelings held for ransom

•

price?

•

(a little weak, a little envious)

•

reading the Iliad

What else is there?

•

I'd like to know her opinion on bones.

•

(can't get enough)

•

overcast

•

cobbled?

•

Black is what everyone in Greece is wearing today, like you, I say.

•

some quip about a blind therapist

•

three days, an eternity

•

We talked about roots and rootlessness and she smiled when I

•

Now it makes me cry.

•

fighting the gods

•

a little reluctant to leave this high nest

•

a blind woman touching her child's face

•

We keep talking about death and graves and cremation and

•

So much of the work occurs in the interstices.

•

I resuscitate myself, imagining.

wake up at all hours of the night, write things down

may go swimming

•

Things have switched a little.

•

We talk about sex and death, death and sex, curiosity and
excitement, arousal and rogue bits of stimulation.

•

As the beloved, one feels a little snatched at.

•

Maybe it's all just an idea.

•

We talked non-stop about customs, superstition, burial, belief.
Green entered the conversation.

•

Yesterday, my mother was wretched.

•

just read an Amichai love poem in Hebrew

read it again

•

Sudafed made me euphoric.

•

When I realized that I would see my son, my chest expanded with
an unexpected but not unfamiliar happiness.

•

slept until daylight

•

I was supposed to be reading the paper.

•

still negotiating this territory

•

all this attempt to look at

•

An icon, come to life.

•

stop narrating?

•

Sometimes you need to put the computer—all computers—aside.

•

sun directly at me

•

My mother says: I'm so scared today.

•

It takes a word, with an emphasis on tone more than meaning to calm her.

Would any set of syllables do?

•

memorizing her?

Her face is so much more than I can imagine.

•

A human being in the room changes the nature of the sacrifice.

•

(Is that what H.D. meant?)

•

sometimes an attic in the house of you, sometimes a basement

•

slit throat, pull skin from flesh, wrap thighbone in fat

fire the scent skyward

•

they're always hungry

•

insinuate mind into the shape of a life, shatter it
make your offering: head on a platter

•

anything to win their favor

•

After a downpour, it's perfectly sunny.

•

It makes me sick how much I love her.

•

Putting on my coat, I say: I wish I could stay here forever.

•

She is older than I thought.

•

Something akin to nausea: the thought of losing her fills me with
dread.

•

Just like this strange weather.

•

I talk to her all day and night.
Arriving, I am mute.

•

She is still capable of surprising—and delighting—me.

•

When our bodies are in the same room, she says.

•

treated her like a mother, acted like a teenager

•

She says: It's too painful.

I nod.

•

Today, like a book, she seemed to be all about love and sadness.

•

There are things to tell her—there always will be.

•

We still see eye-to-eye.

•

5 a.m., first street car rattles through

•

Will you last long enough?

•

(Will you last?)

•

She shines her motherly light on me and I bask in it.

•

live the days, sew them up

•

I know saints—I definitely know a saint or two.

•

The truth of the matter is that this is where I live.

•

When she said "poetry," I balked.

•

I don't want to escape—I want to live at the heart of it.

in its heart

in her heart

•

Does she have any questions for me?

•

Who cares about fiction, anyway?

•

You think it's nostalgia—the meat, the sacrifices, the rocky land
and sea—but really, they're right here.

•

Those curtains change color with the light.

•

Meditated this morning. First thing.

•

sex—a distant tease

•

an Achilles, clanging around in his armor

Agamemnon, the buffoon in the corner

•

I don't know how she did it.

I did it, I suppose.

•

Coax it alive by thinking it right?

•

arousal? eros

•

We aim to be Athenas but mostly devolve into Heras.

Hera: jealous bitch with white arms

•

Aphrodite?

•

aim for the stump, not the log

•

Last night, I read the word "asshole" and lit up through to my intestines.

•

(So the revelation here is language?)

•

As he did what he did, I began to narrate.

•

Detoxified guilt is—pleasure?

•

And then I was desperate to continue marking spots, digging a pin against the sky, punctuating something—my existence— puncturing it?

•

ever-anxious of audience

•

written words, including sex

•

frightened by and enamored of spoken words

•

You spend time with a person—you make an impression.

(you take one home)

•

the body, invented by language

•

Words tame it; words may urge it wild.

•

You're right: Some part of me thinks—*knows*—I'll die together with her.

•

too much talk, too much *chatter*

•

buy the clothes

(don't cut the hair)

•

approaching muteness

•

(still jabbering)

•

I'm not done—I haven't even started.

•

in a frenzy to finish

•

(stay ahead of the debt)

•

headache up my right side: neck to cheekbone

•

incapable of procuring her

•

I keep failing, somehow, in that room.

•

(reinvent her?)

•

I handed it all to her on a (paper) platter.

•

bumbling along

•

When she dies, I will go silent?
When he dies, the world will go silent?

•

I should go out and do something.

•

Just wrote a kind of love letter to that new friend, but chaste.

•

Make life seem normal by mimicking it when it was.

•

This is what I like to do.

(sit here and write)

•

In some sense, her use of language is only as good as mine.

•

I guess there's that thing between us

•

small black, orange-breasted birds
green hills, raindrops
a form of buttercup I'm not familiar with

•

Womb?
(cervix)

•

grapevines (like living graves)
bristle of vineyard
ubiquitous cows

•

One of these days I'll say: So let's talk about Greece.

•

What were those words she twinned?

•

greens and hard-boiled eggs for dinner

•

mangled vulture, dog, deer

•

Do you agree that I've become timid—or is that just where we
are?

•

nostos, even as I walk these streets, pave this time now

•

For each new audience, a turn?

•

(can't risk boring her)

•

I could read a book.

•

This is thinking poetically?

•

It has not ceased to amaze

•

sucking echinacea from a dropper

•

yesterday his birthday, today the grave

•

westerly whistling through

•

(a line at a time)

•

not repeatable: whole cloth

•

My sister's office is a little like an art gallery; hers is like a womb.

•

I sat on the floor putting the world back together in jigsaw pieces.

•

I guess I can continue to go forward.

•

The cemetery will be gloomy today—that's the weather.

•

loath to give up that nimbus, symbiosis

•

Something budged!

•

desire, like bright tracers, up and down the length of me

•

not good at quieting myself

•

raining, happily so!

•

all those Poles, dead on Russian soil

There's tragedy for you, a he-goat song.

•

Goats that are mine by virtue of proximity.

Occasionally their young follow me—hopeful, sure—until they're not.

They bolt toward a goatier version of me.

•

eyes like hands? (mine reach, hers hold)

•

I will not give up this trope.

•

No longer sickened by it, I can withstand the adoration of my mother's reaching eyes

•

childlike, vulnerable and watching

•

Does meditation kill the vital energies?

•

(fuck that eastern bullshit)

•

billowy white clouds

•

nothing wrong with a little pleasure, is there?

•

We saw the grave of a Carl Jung today, but it wasn't THE Carl Jung.

•

No monuments, she would say, if she could understand.

•

Strange cypresses, and then a whole conversation about trees.

•

no sun to speak of, just sons

•

Breathing still does it.

•

Like those trees, I'm a little bowed under by it.

•

"The bright-eyed Pallas lost no time. Down she flashed from the peaks of Mount Olympus, quickly reached the ships and found

Odysseus first, a mastermind like Zeus..."

•

in awe of it, or whatever made it

•

Whoever?

•

the perennial problem: what to take, what to leave behind

•

intermittent rain, just when you thought

•

stretches of pavement dotted with wet pink petals

•

cloudy sky, pale blue

•

Those red carnations at the cemetery: an employee came through with a bucket.

•

I read that female porcupines sometimes walk around with a stick between their legs.

•

waiting for my passport—it could be any minute

•

Sometimes when I laugh, my father's dead mother is laughing with me.

•

Have I done my duty? Am I allowed to leave now?

•

solipsism?

•

(may sometimes have its uses)

•

Yesterday, my mother was back to calling me her mother.

•

Today, even the shortest book seems too long.

•

break out of this cave?

•

(stay in it forever)

•

There's the crux, the cross.

•

There is a you.
(A you has broken in.)

•

drinking a glass of it, alone

•

She said it was epic, in its way.

•

Once, I thought I was good at this.

•

Today, she was angry. Or was that me?

•

Eros and death: the themes that suck me in and drink me down.

•

I have been drunk—by others and another.

•

(Will it always boil down to a mother and a child?)

•

I think she was talking about the need even an analyst feels to pull rabbits out of a hat.

•

It's giving me something like a headache.

•

trying to go deep and

•

epic, in a way

•

still being written (of course)

•

She said: Are you going to tell me what's going on?

•

(called me a half-nomad)

•

Will my fucking passport get here in time?

•

a glass of wine for dinner

•

all this, a little excruciating

•

(can't abide sexlessness)

•

All night, I think of the raw and the cooked as if a concept can provide a way out of a dilemma.

•

She returned my call immediately.

•

(can't call her anything)

•

I stepped off the treadmill and lay on the floor, stretching and crying, stretching and crying.

•

We need to talk about names.

•

The compulsion to avoid naming the sacred recurs at critical junctures?

•

My friend killed a porcupine in the middle of the night. Twelve bashes with a thick branch of pine. When she got back into bed, she couldn't stop thinking of Rodney King.

•

I love a hard sexual clenching.

•

Yesterday, she said: So are you going to tell me what's going on?

•

I bring the outside world in, then banish it?

•

these odd (mortifying) forces

•

We hugged at the cemetery; I cried small sobs against him.

•

spreading myself thin?

•

Cut my pubic hair this morning.

•

After an eternity of silence, I said: I don't know how to proceed.

•

We flirt.
I flit.
(She traps me in a net of her ingenious invention.)

•

I look at her face, negotiating the distance.
There's nothing erotic here now: I'm trying to turn air to liquid.

•

dying of some thirst or other

•

(blessed cool touch)

•

I am a pilgrim at the shrine of her.

•

I say: I've used up all my tricks.
She says: Maybe they're not tricks at all.

•

(My sister texts: You've brought Mom back to life!)

•

My sister's face is thin but beautiful.

•

about to breathe so hard I had to look away

•

Where the *hell* is my passport?

•

She works her seduction, I work mine.

•

She said: It was after you'd given up your secret.

•

(self-display, self-immolation)

•

I keep saying subterranean but I may actually mean submerged.

•

a Starbucks cup beside her

•

Once I empty myself with telling you, I will be able to think abroad?

•

Here in the postmodern age, I write myself raw.

•

Bold!

I lit up—everywhere—then turned away to recompose.

•

People on the street are wearing shorts and sandals.

•

I love her avidly, chronically.

•

She said: It's amazing.

Don't you know that?

•

New York—is that her accent?

•

(Life begins again.)

•

I'll be a river, if you'll have me flow by.

•

She said it again: You tricked and seduced me. It's amazing.

•

I'd been at the very bottom of my barrel.

•

(One more time, please, so the words on your voice will stick in the suitcase of my heart?)

•

A black man, grizzled white beard, missing teeth, came to the door in a 49ers shirt, asking for money for the Tenderloin breakfast program. I gave him $20; he gave me a piece of paper.

•

She said she thought I'd said outlawed words.

•

(roam, eyes)

•

We always say hello and goodbye twice.

•

I loved that man, almost immediately.

•

(I hit the mark of her, the heart of her, the beam I'd aimed to touch.)

•

The sun—I keep neglecting the weather.

•

I bought party clothes yesterday—a whole slew of them.

•

Wrote in a frenzy, while driving to my mother's house, in a little blue notebook.

•

(constantly speaking to you)

•

I keep playing it over: the words on her voice from her face.

•

What are the exact physics of desire?

•

monumental clenching

•

I expect punishment when I admit love?

•

I nodded, which is all I seem to do these days, with you, and mouthed a yes in your direction.

•

Chicago in winter. We used that luxurious bed; we left our imprint on that mattress, those fine sheets.

•

So, I have your permission to continue?

•

For women who have adored their mothers, attracting men is not a problem.

•

That man zeroed in on me; he walked over leisurely.

•

this sacrifice, this gentle (abrupt) slit in the vein of me—a steady trickle out toward you, unstoppable, it seems, until I will have stopped

•

Did I ever tell you that I look like both my parents?

•

(She gave me her body.)

•

She said: You're always watching the clock.

•

(this compulsion to kiss time)

•

When I couldn't find another thing inside, she opened her hands.

•

What do you call those trees?

•

(You filled in the blank.)

•

I keep that picture on my table: my three, the harbor, the water.

•

In some sense, all words are outlaws. Just, words at all, sometimes need to be outlawed.

•

She loosens my tongue, and then she doesn't.

•

A line I love: oomerachok mayteem she'ayn lehakiram. "And from afar, unrecognizable dead."

•

For a week, my tea had no taste.

•

broccolini steaming downstairs

tired

•

In the Iliad, even minor characters are fully realized.

A couple of thousand years later and more, I write myself, alone.

•

Love finds many forms; you can't not call it love.

•

Lost another New York City earring—down the drain.

•

My mother thinks her legs—or her pants?—are people, places, things, and sometimes ideas.

•

fierce grace, that new friend's words

•

I asked if she had children, attempting boldness.

•

And retreat to this other, this discreet, this sexual vein.

•

Leaving, it's as if I'm dying, all the places go on without me.

Negative transference?

Positive?

•

Sisters are born each with the other's tongue in her mouth; the two duel for ascendancy over everything tasted and said.

•

She moves her head to flip the hair, a chosen color, and looking at you—but not quite seeing you—she says: I bow to no one.

•

messages

•

this state of almost-bloody vulnerability and surrender, a baby in its (adoring?) mother's arms

•

She, of course, usurped my place, but we've been in this thing practically forever.

•

sun a smudge behind the clouds

•

Side by side on treadmills, I told my sister that I'd always known our mother's death would require recompense.

She looked at me; I wasn't sure if I read awe or distaste, maybe a little of each, or neither.

•

Once, for my sister, I picked up a hard little mouse.

•

With the world raised to your lips, you'll give your sister anything, any piece of yourself that will bring her closer than the close you already share.

•

(keeping a thing in the dark doesn't necessarily keep it alive)

•

I covet the crow's *click*, more human invention than bird.

•

stayed up past midnight, filling small bottles from larger ones

creating essences?

•

(I hear myself saying the words aloud as I type them. *Incanting*?)

•

A husband, at least as much as a wife, contains.

But my husband, container, spills the contents of our mixing.

•

(together, we spill)

•

A cloud of ash between us, as well as an ocean and a sea. There's no taking a train from here to there, no bus or taxi to him.

•

I love her small "uh-huh," more note than word, both prod and touch.

•

She picked up the piece, began.

She handed it to me.

•

Then we went back into the material.

•

The plum tree in the front—quiet. The lavender—insatiable. The lilac, almost hostile it's so beautiful.

•

My mother laughed almost hysterically, in a happy confusion over the volcanic ash in the sky and my mother-in-law's ashes, in an urn.

•

When we stood to say goodbye, she put her hands behind her back. They are tied, I suppose, by the rules of her profession.

One day, perhaps, we'll touch hands in honor of what has passed between us.

•

lighter than air and weighted as the earth

•

How much hunger can a person stand?

•

There are times when you avoid chocolate to make way for more absorbing pleasures.

•

(desire adores a vacuum)

•

Then I launched into the island story about the dynamite going off at the wrong time, killing four.

•

a kiss without touching?

•

The only way to tell a story is by taking time and slicing it.

•

A sister's body may catch between you and any number of motions; her gestures may kill.

•

Notice how you've become a volcano, always spewing. For now, it's the hot lava of longing and desire.

Later, ash?

•

Spewing? Or offering up every good thing I have to the only deity I know?

•

Wait, I tell my sister. *Listen!*

•

She says: You're on *fire*!

•

I keep getting caught between a sentence and a kiss.

•

I ask him: *Do you think you're the only one with a little lava on your sleeve?*

•

to go *beyond* perfection

•

This is *my* body?

•

streetcar just came to life

•

holding onto everything you want to let go: (archery?)

•

She may not be doing it on purpose but the fact is, it taunts.

•

Every time I fall just short of sleep, a mouth is there to meet mine.

•

two open mouths breathing warm currents

•

Sitting does it, breathing insists on it (my body insists on breathing), eating, thinking about eating, waiting for the water to boil, looking out the window, lilac, washing lettuce, sitting down, standing up, walking—everything a signpost upon this door, my body.

•

the tongue's tip, searching for a path

•

(defining it)

•

Her mouth held my words; she offered them to the world on the breath of her.

•

A mouth, and another mouth, each a perfect everything.

•

She says: You're the exhibitionist, I'm the voyeur.

•

I tend to be gathered in the arms of one excitement or another.

•

(often squeezed breathless)

•

There are ways of talking about secrets, ways of telling them.

•

naked, flipping our skin off, and on again

•

My mother is in the water of the Bay, though she never learned to swim. She's in the hills that set our vision at an angle as we look toward the water, sparkling in this April day's sun.

•

A week ago it was pouring—we were at the cemetery.

•

Does a shared secret remain a secret?

•

(A secret gains potency by being told?)

•

That scenario: he dies of pleasure, I kill him with love.

•

I share the fact and object of my love, unable to contain it.

•

She said: Like, once a day?
Yes.
A little shy to add, *at least*. Or: *No, one hundred times!*

•

Every time I think of her, I bloom, then wilt.

•

(How did she make it happen?)

•

She is some perfection.

•

(He could take a lesson.)

•

the terror of losing her and every woman contained in her,
including the her of me

•

No wonder my stomach hurts.

•

Everything out there—siren, streetcar, lamp, plum tree—
penetrates my fear, giving birth to me.

•

She remains the world, increasingly.

•

The wind, hardly a moan, tortures a window of the house, and me
inside it.

•

I told her: She was fine today, herself, normal, *amazing*.

•

(My sister said: *You've brought her back to life!*)

•

Tapped at the source, this thing won't stop or be stopped up.

•

this writing—pure sickness, or health

•

sideshow, freak, fact of nature, phenomenon

•

The deaths of the fathers were nothing compared to this birth-
giving life watched fading, glowing, burning brighter than

•

Your ears fill up with tears—you take them for the sea.

•

an impossible combination of grief and love

•

With no you, I, alone, write myself against the plane that holds
me.

•

half a Xanax for terror?

•

She and I are not the same patient; we are not the same girl.

•

(Sex and words spew from me, alternating.)

•

on the bed in the house in the city whose streets are abandoning
my feet

•

When did she get so beautiful?

•

We reeled, we waltzed, we sashayed.

We shouted bright code across the apples and pears.

•

En route to LA. The sun is up.

•

to confess the secret and still be thundered by its power

•

(Secrets, revealed, may turn river.)

•

Sisters, with their good legs and aging beautiful faces.

•

He has nothing against letting me surround him.

The plane is still asleep, but I can smell syrup.

•

Certain of her, I can proceed.

•

Learning to be explicit about panic?

•

This flight holds me, this flight contains her.

•

Waiting for coffee, tea. Anything.

•

Tomorrow, we sprinkle her ashes. Sprinkle? Bury? Dust?

•

midnight espresso?

•

We're all a chemical sluice that will one day turn to ash.

•

Tomorrow, down on earth, she, all ash, will mix with earth, less pure but quick.

•

the sky, filled with ash, filling up with mothers

•

Maybe she's right: poetry.

•

language: edible

•

They're folding the blankets.

Window shades are up.

•

Turbulence.

Is that ash?

•

my bright Scandinavian-colored sister!

•

Crossing the boot—breakfast?

•

Be well!

•

gaining on Greece

•

Forgiveness?

•

Odysseus' islands. Aimed now toward Troy. Passing Crete.

•

I cry a little, 35,000 feet up.

•

(closer to the God we claim we don't believe in)

•

language, an ecstasy

•

not even a smidgen of a headache, not a particle

•

turned on by grammar, too

•

Is this perversity or just a life?

•

(Mediterranean beneath cloud)

•

She wrote: I was afraid.

I wrote: So was I.

She wrote: Of what?

Of myself in relation to you.

•

To end hostility in the being of you: no banking small hurts or tiny woes.

•

Wherever here is, I am also there.

•

How to navigate without drowning in a hostile sea?

•

human quills

Chopped salad the way they do it here, the way I like it.

•

2 a.m.

ruminations in a new time zone

•

Do I dare cross oceans in thought?

•

I walked in the wadi so long they came out looking for me.

•

One mosquito—it's the same story anywhere.

•

Sometimes a gong sounds: loneliness reverberates.

•

What one seems to want is the eyes of an other.

•

breath: sustenance

•

(a meal)

•

Admit weakness; the world floods in.

•

Five a.m., raucous birds.

•

I've begun to remember my mother?

•

The dog just opened the door. Clever Jewish dogs.

•

Now, any occasion is cause for tears.

•

We drove past camels and Arab villages, the wall by our side.

•

No longer afraid of lone Arab terrorists lurking beneath my bed, I walk naked in the dark.

•

the sky today? white, hazy, cloudy

•

slipping into the language, less infiltrator than citizen?

•

having procured a kind of mother, reminiscent of what she may once have been

•

dried figs, dates, tahini, tuna from a can

Something in me wants fish.

•

Inbar, an ugly name with a strange beauty, means: tongue of the bell.

•

difficult texts

•

repeating everything I hear, like a child, attempting to lock it in

•

Can't wait to get to Nicosia, can't wait to get back to Jerusalem.

•

Kafrisim. Kritim. Islands.

•

my tongue has loosened

•

rain

•

The dogs have finally stopped barking.

•

Was that great-grandfather hiding in a closet to avoid the Cossacks?

•

rain, but lighter now

•

in another language

•

This is what it feels like to be forgotten?

•

my mother, afar

•

Sore nipples and they're not yet in his mouth.

•

At Ben Gurion, I sip an espresso while men huddle by windows facing east, davening beneath their tallitot.

•

dawn

•

this (ever-seductive) language, the new movements it forces on my tongue and lips, the forms it insists I master

•

Sleep will be a welcome guest.

•

closer to putting my finger on the source

•

a mare in a woman's body

•

a desert between time zones

•

Every time I close my eyes, I'm at the peak of an ascent.

•

At the moshav gate at three in the morning, the shomer, the guard, offered me a cup of tea and when I refused, handed me a sprig of lemon verbena.

•

fragrant!

•

That Haredi is praying, but my compass says he's facing west.

•

Or am I terrified that someone will steal this magic?

maimed: such a rush of blood!

•

We're burying my mother-in-law's ashes at the cemetery, just before closing time, just before sunset.

•

trowel, gloves, gravel

•

mourners?

•

here, so close to Paphos, where Aphrodite rose from the sea

•

thank you

•

muse?

•

time to go down and meet the (funeral?) party

•

Three months to the day, I just came alive.

•

gravel?

•

here in the land of round hay bales and Aphrodites rising from sea foam

•

sing a muse?

•

(The song of it's the mingling.)

•

To the west: billowy but focused; to the east: faded, possibly tempestuous.

•

a muse is a muse

•

(feminine and perfect)

•

peopled by voices

•

dialogue, quartet, symphony

•

(jug band, snore)

•

This quick talk makes sparks.

•

sharp arrows

•

you may be right

•

romantic wounds

•

define muse

•

I suckle him to clarity, this moment.

•

even old, diminished without their mother

•

middle of the Cypriot night

•

Apparently I can't escape this heat, this rise, my heart.

•

(brain a little clogged)

•

rising violently against him

•

(aiming for the moon)

•

I rise against his subtle hand

•

Where are you in the mix of family and sinners?

•

(no saints)

•

I believe we come here for the salt.

•

(salt of his past, the spice of it)

•

my mother, astray

•

My brain is stiff, my eyes and neck

•

working up an appetite

•

with a plane of time behind us?

•

these quick shots (espresso)

•

Cyprus—small, dry, dear

•

I touched the bits of bone, not ash at all but tiny crumb-like
stones.

•

He crumbled, too, like bone, but wet.

•

It had rained and the graves—the surrounding grass and earth—
were alive.

•

Giving up exhaustion, I give you up—one version.

•

so much food left on the table

•

(salt)

•

talk of summer plans, memories of heat

•

some great hunger, surfacing

•

Hunger creeps into the mouth.

•

That woman says: *epidi den thaftike…*

•

(because she wasn't buried)

•

no sister left to mourn her

•

what remains

•

The hats she eats are bitter.

•

mixed in with the humus of her husband?

•

(each good fuck begs (for) another)

•

No one mourns purely; there are additives.

•

belief between the legs?

•

with the hope of clean sacrifice, extended bloodletting

•

seeking beauty

-

present in the rhythm?

-

It turns out: those ashes were heavy.

-

(My constant heavy breathing: he laughs)

-

an epic of sorts

-

reviving the you in me

-

a kind of Helen: a mist, a fog, a veil, a screen

-

inspiration: a breath

-

(but sharp, inhaled against one's will)

-

No doubt, my sister's right: exhibitionism.

-

She said: But, like everyone, you have your blind spots.

-

Cyprus is soft, feminine, a good place to birth a goddess.

-

having gone a little dead

-

exquisite surrender

•

(I bob there, stupid with it.)

•

That part has been sealed.

•

Don't think I don't think of my mother: I do.

•

O, Muse

•

Epic. You said it.

•

write toward ecstasy?

•

like a Maenad, mad to tear him to pieces

•

A shot of espresso jump-starts the day.

•

(Anticipation jump-starts the moment.)

•

inspiration—a fist to the heart, a kick to the loins

•

tonight, Jerusalem

•

a coupling that fertilizes the mind that spawns the seeds?

•

a special breath?

•

You will do anything, you will take small and large risks.

•

Ache at the heart of you: it hardly lets up.

•

half-packed suitcases

•

those plastic cards that work as keys: a careless collection

•

perfection: a full cup, *tilting*

•

We come here to eat salty things and revel in the tricky, clever twists of Cypriot.

•

ravished by a muse

•

only one weather and it's internal

•

After digging the ash of their mother into a sad bit of earth beside the grave, we gathered the tools—saw, knife, trowel—and walked the narrow path between the graves back toward the entrance.

•

In the taxi, we named the muses: Erato, Melpomene, Kalliope, Euterpe, Ourania, Terpsichore, Thalia, Kleio, Polyhymnia.

•

Erato being the one

•

swam twice today

•

ate pligouri

•

Instructions for a nap: Hold a set of keys in your hand, sit back. When the keys fall from your hand, the nap is over.

•

worried, eating almonds

•

spread me?

•

Flying into Ben Gurion at midnight, I close my eyes.

•

Good bed at the King David. Good sheets.

•

any which way

•

(distasteful?)

•

There are so many ways to surrender.

•

unable to walk away from what's hanging around inside

•

the amount of psychological traction necessary to allow this degree of surrender?

•

a sudden, sharp longing for San Francisco

•

something good to eat

•

give up the self of me for a political shell?

•

Change comes unbidden (or with great heaving effort).

•

I wonder what San Francisco is doing right now.

•

One finger displaced a life?

•

removed the world from Axis' shoulders?

•

freed it to tumble, gather speed?

•

We now have a history of being this way.

•

(voracious)

•

These parts enter the discussion; these parts have a seat at the table.

•

Miraculously, even with stinger out, that bite still swells.

•

pluck

That politican—kind of a jerk, kind of a jock—turned out to be a pretty good dancer.

•

(We almost dropped our party dresses to the floor.)

•

introduction to politics:

•

high common ground "*shared*"?

•

(beware the annihilating embrace)

•

I have no voice in these matters.

•

song to speechlessness in thirty seconds!

•

The complexity of the situation is apt to render one speechless.

•

(no excuse)

•

There are countless ways to speak of this piece of geography.

•

(countless ways to offend)

•

Biblical?

-

political resonance in the naming

-

Messianic?

-

(silent and loquacious, both)

-

Though many still hadn't finished their coffee, their permits were about to expire.

-

I am part of a delegation?

-

We kept driving around in circles. Our understanding followed a similar circuity; it was impossible to know exactly where we were.

-

Noting that the word "occupation" has become fashionable, this man says he is particularly moved as he walks the path trod by King David at the Cave of the Patriarchs.

-

think Baruch Goldstein

-

(The concept of shame predates Freud—and Judaism, for that matter.)

-

finally made it to the West Bank

-

(a credential, of sorts)

•

couldn't keep my eyes open in the Knesset

•

Our children keep calling us.

They've invented an enemy or merely a rival?

•

in any group, a (negotiable) pecking order

•

Speechlessness lacks power.

•

Silence repudiates it?

•

tongue-tied: sickness

•

a land divided

•

They walk a narrow path along a street that was once theirs, and bustling.

•

Hold out both arms: this hand touches one side, that hand the other.

•

look up: wire netting to catch tossed garbage

•

We walked freely, with large, leisurely strides.

•

Enchanting or disgusting, it's a show that requires evaluation.

•

Muammar's father, once the mayor of Hebron, considered a collaborator, shot dead.

•

(a complicated legacy for a six-year-old)

•

Each of those men lost a brother to the conflict.

•

(think Gandhi and King)

•

revenge, an idea they've eschewed

•

Onions, he says, are more important than schoolbooks.

•

(combat the effect of tear gas)

•

If you can't see for the tears, what good are the books?

•

(so natural to seek an eye for an eye)

•

almost impossible to imagine the strength

•

the life going out of a brother

•

banishing vengeance

-

heroic

-

One of them said: "Let's not call it peace, let's call it normal."

-

Near the Erez Crossing into Gaza, an army officer tells us that he's been inside a house filled with sand.

-

Whose narrative are you spouting now?

-

(she asks herself)

-

I/thou: compact

-

self-contained

-

(God-in-a-self)

-

Where are you, *Eli*?

-

(no God, just gods)

-

caffeine: self-contained-dialogue-inducing

-

sentimental to say that I loved Hebron?

-

criminal?

•

simply foolish?

•

the warmth of the underdog?

•

(won't speak of victims)

•

(I've noticed that) I tend not to listen when I should.

•

I love trading glances.

•

being seen

•

(exhibitionist?)

•

(think of) the lives not seen

•

lived under the sky

•

a sea of languages, combined and heaving, shoots skyward in a
fireworks of splash and utterance

•

then falls

•

(gravity holds, even with words, *milim*)

- always running after a consummation

- seeking one orgasm or another

- climax: the name of the game

- Last night, I could have pursued him and been pursued—nimble, hunted, hunter—for hours, mesmerized by what was unfolding, in thrall to what would come.

- Erez Crossing: No one crosses?

- less than half a dozen people waiting to get through a huge, empty, technologically sophisticated immigration center

- An old woman sits on the ground, takes off her shoes.

- We're told that, like us, the 1.5 million people living in Gaza are students, businessmen, professors, doctors, social workers, and farmers.

- "Peaceman" blogs from Gaza; "Hopeman" blogs from Sderot.

- The houses on this kibbutz are neat; palm trees sway.

- He points toward the sea behind us: waste goes directly into the Mediterranean.

•

She tells us that when a Qassam is fired, you have to make quick decisions: Whose child do I take off the bus first?

•

Mine? Someone else's?

•

(whose?)

•

out of the blue, a supersonic sound bomb!

•

(We all jump a little.)

•

"Only a normal life will foster more moderate opinion" is a lot like saying, "Let's not call it peace, let's call it normal."

•

"The unsung heroes," he says, "are the ambulance drivers who drive straight into the line of fire in order to pick up the wounded." "Straight into it," he says, pale skin ruddy with emotion, black hair. Irish.

•

"We're not there to make excuses for failure."

•

How to inscribe the lesson in their hearts?

•

(eighteen bullets in the side of his car)

•

The border stays closed; the underground economy stays open.

•

8,000 five-year-olds waiting to go to the UN schools

•

He reminds us not to be naïve.

•

painfully silent, but by psychological inclination, not political restriction

•

(a world of difference)

•

(You could venture to say that this is an exercise, examining silence in the face of eloquence—but you would be wrong.)

•

When the microphone comes close, all I want is for it to pass.

•

luxury? insolence? stupidity?

•

Doesn't everyone covet the possession of a voice?

•

(I turn it down)

•

(coward)

•

How is a hero made?

•

Camus: "Between my mother and justice, I prefer my mother."

•

I looked up and saw Arafat grinning above us.

•

Caught myself saying: "He seems determined to deliver."

•

(Is there no way to protect oneself from this language?)

•

language, and whether you're willing to let your mind be changed by it

•

these politicians, thinkers, human rights organizers: objects of desire

•

(Can't toss the sexual model?)

•

(Isn't that the bulk of politics, anyway?)

•

Wearing my king-and-queen outfit today: black suit with off-white silk blouse. Black pearl earrings.

•

(shoes: Lanvin)

•

last night: dinner outside of Amman looking over the Jordan Valley

•

miles of lights down to the Dead Sea

•

notes on index cards

•

(important? useless?)

•

that kite, flying high above Ramallah!

•

We're back from the palace.

•

They're talking about the state of the world; I'm thinking about my husband's mouth.

•

Notes:

If you think it through, it's very easy to solve; if you start with rhetoric, it doesn't work.

incrementally but systematically

("Negotiation" is a dirty word.)

in contravention not only of the Geneva Convention but of signed agreements

Rescue peace from the jaws of war.

serious brain drain

systematic assault on democracy and people's individual rights

the ugliest border in the world

The ratio of security to freedom is a political decision.

what the average American doesn't know

•

fence?

•

wall

•

that man's grandfather, killed in '49 while trying to raise a white flag

•

(left a wife and seven kids)

•

this road—used only by settlers and internationals

•

(Saying you're not taking a side is, of course, taking a side.)

•

The archaeologist told us that he seeks to practice an enlightened science based on empirical data, not Bible stories.

•

2006: half the wall complete

2006: last year in which suicide bombers came into Israel

•

half a wall?

•

Homemade rockets have a short shelf life.

•

a silent exhibitionist?

•

no words, only a kite rising higher and higher

•

drinking water, eating hummus

•

Only through the body's fine-tuning can the mind come through. (You could say the opposite—it works both ways.)

•

Knowing the language wasn't necessary: I could tell from the buzz, the hum, and the way they looked at each other that the thing had worked.

But I *did* understand what those fifteen-year-olds were saying: "We discovered that we're almost the same."

•

grape leaves just past my eye

•

(I love this place.)

•

only the odd poem, and in Hebrew

•

Here in Jerusalem, traffic passes to the east, to the north; I look out on a valley.

•

scare my husband with the ferocity of my appetite

•

Warmed by wine, we made friends with husband-and-wife police officers. My husband is amazed; I'm not willing to be so.

•

These windows reflect us back at ourselves. What a surprise.

•

this incidence of self-revelation, self-stimulation

•

(self-saturation?)

•

I've written about language, I've written about tongues.

•

all of life, merely rehearsal for the end?

•

back in Jerusalem with light pouring into this home within a building, once a Christian hospital

•

finally slept more than four hours

•

The traffic outside is relentless but the view is magnificent.

•

spoke to one son from Amman, the other from Jerusalem

•

bells before 7, the wild, Greek kind

•

across a valley, graves on a hill beneath cypresses, like ours

•

hungry!

•

(starving)

•

okay, meditate

•

rebellion? discreet challenge? (discrete?)

●

birds, traffic, Arabic

jasmine, geranium, grape

●

To be alive; my mother waxes nostalgic.

●

today, a nourishing day

●

tea again, a saving grace

●

That Arab woman thanked me.

●

Our children sense that our new interest in saving the world has
made our interest in them wane, a little.

●

always alert to the scent of smoke

●

Is that an easterly?

●

fingers to mouth toward the gesture of a kiss

●

The crows here steal food from plates when people turn away.

●

haven't called my mother once

●

Last night, I said, I'm going to meditate now, and did, right next to him, his breath mingling with mine, the pages of his newspaper turning, as my body did, in the acquiescence it seems to have captured now.

•

I've never been reticent, but the well of feeling has deepened.

•

stomach a little flabby?

•

out there, graves

•

almost always ready

•

(porn not intended!)

•

slowly dwindling light, sky pure of cloud

•

bursting into a new season

•

your fingers, one by one

•

those graves—most likely ancient

•

Not enough hours in the day; I steal some from the night.

•

(living in two time zones)

•

The insides of my mouth are a little bitten up.

•

A couple of times, in downtown Ramallah, he looked back to make sure I was there.

•

beginning to make sense of Arabic syllables

•

my first schwarma

•

I keep imagining meaning onto the syllables.

•

out the window: dawn

•

A recording of the muezzin came on over a speaker.

•

Just a few more notes:

You cannot stop someone who has lost the fear of death.

At the palace, the king said that moderate Arab statesmen sit around the table texting each other. (The extremists have yet to figure it out.)

The queen said: "We have failed to humanize this conflict."

•

garbage and small fires at Qualandya

•

The sense of something monumental about to happen at the checkpoint; we passed through with ease.

•

(there, too)

•

challas means enough

•

What gust have you caught?

•

a plethora of tongues

•

dividing the land of us

•

(corners, walls, plains)

•

(an abundance of names)

•

aloft

•

not exactly queasy

KADDISH

Need to put things in order, take a walk on a treadmill, translate something.

Be translated.

What I would really like to do? Write between the lines.

•

The sky is mute—nothing blue to it; the sea is immense and calm.

We discovered that the peahen had been sitting on hollow eggs.

This is my way of speaking (to you), almost in the present tense.

•

Thirty seconds of rain.

Roses: dollops of frosting.

•

Ate chocolate. Came back to life.

•

Touching you from an uncanny distance.

•

Walked to the beach at noon, swam, then back up the long hill.

Lunch was grilled food—my husband, my chef. Then the food we make of each other.

•

(this lively animation)

•

Cats prowl in the vines above the roses.

Writing makes the present.

•

What meditation does? Stretches time. Digs into it?

•

A god: procured in full knowledge?

•

Just: emptiness surrounding the hemispheres.

•

Always mosquitoes now. Mid-May.

•

But one need not be wedded to silence!

•

You understand: to escape awareness of time only to have it burst upon you at odd moments.

•

An audible syllable—the only outcome of that journey.

•

I'm breathing for you.

•

There are levels and levels of intimacy. You never know

•

Look at, not back?

•

His ego (may squash mine).

•

To bear sexual witness. Is there such a thing?

•

Figure out a way to shine it home.

•

He is cooking for me, I am exposing him in a piece I can't stop sacrificing on the altar of my body.

But this gift is for him, simmering.

•

Putting your money where your mouth is. (always a gamble)

•

Here, now, tomato sauce that's been cooking for over an hour. It's the cinnamon that fills the house and makes you think you might be hungry, even if you know you're not.

This is my husband's doing. And then it begins again.

Cut to politics?

•

As a child, I loved these long, almost-summer days. Now, I'm more interested in the dark before dawn.

•

Just. Lust.

•

Fine, now. We are fine, and I have resolved my

•

Begin with generosity (as a value) and see where you stumble.

•

The birds go crazy when we fuck.

•

In the stew, stirring things around, whisking things together. Tasting.

I can turn away from this concoction and you're still there looking at me.

•

Huge gusts of wind between pauses.

•

(And your sexual greed? Where do you place it on a continuum?)

•

I watch that line of ants, arduously, marchingly carry a piece of something we neglected to put in our mouths.

•

Pulled so taut by time, I'm almost always

•

Someone just arrived noisily, with something. I can hear them stowing it.

•

(the life in the spaces between the sentences)

•

Walked with him through the gorge to the beach.

Swam.

•

Sometimes turn other and inside out.

•

(proofing my galleys)

•

A gull flew over me so directly that I was able to understand just how narrow—like a blade!—a bird makes its body in order to fly.

•

Sucking and weeping, at once.

•

Just: anything that occurs, at any moment.

•

But what I don't want to give up: the theory of your eyes.

•

First cicada! 10:07 a.m., May 29th.

•

Today, he killed two things for me and filled every hole at once.

•

I've learned to make use of translations—backwards and forwards.

•

The crackle of burning wood: he's started dinner.

•

Some insect or other makes sound like a sibilant machine.

•

You have to have Spanish—it goes without saying.

•

Quietly in awe of this thing.

•

Hornets!

•

The excitement of what has been feeding into what may be.

And how touching him is like being touched.

•

Like a woman in a movie, taking the world in through her skin.

•

What about the secrets a person keeps from herself?

Still eager to know the secret at the very heart of the world.

•

On a plane: collected in a ball, in a seat—nowhere to roll. Is that what

•

I can't describe my politics for the life of me.

•

Voted. I can't resist the smell of a school.

•

A voyeur is an exhibitionist in another form?

I've lost my knack, a little.

•

I said: It seems to have become a habit. Habits aren't surprising.

She said: But their motivations are.

•

The UPS truck just sped by—nothing for me.

•

A lover is naked; an artist's model poses in the nude. The writing should seem naked, but the seemingness of it makes it nudity.

•

She's pushing for something but it's not ringing true.

•

Green beans, like zucchini, have something bewitching in their flavor.

•

What do you do with the recalcitrant bits, the parts that want to remain memory, unforged?

•

Once, in a room with an east-facing window, I dug a splinter of wood from my finger.

What is an alien object, lodged?

•

Will the next piece be single words in a vertical line? Hieroglyphical? Written from right to left? Boustrophedon? Palindromic?

•

Sudden sharp pain of missing her. (Mother, the real, still-existing one.)

•

The bed is an object of importance, but so was the fact of gravity that keeps us nailed to the earth.

•

Fleet presences dart around the meditating (bowl of) me.

•

We stood there with others who, like us, wanted their standing to count as a shout, a clamor, a drum, a fist, (tears). Invigorating and sad (a bit of a letdown) to be at the heart of a conflict, almost on TV.

•

What I've returned to? The rest of the world.

•

I took the clothes to the cleaners; they'll be washed free of the air that blew through the days—jasmine, (hint of) gunpowder.

•

just: scared

•

That old woman? Half-buried, already.

We're just waiting to drop another shovelful.

(But, a parent's demise does not render adult a child.)

Wretched today.

•

Haven't seen any animals other than pigeons, dogs, and cats in over a week.

•

I learned the word for flotilla (*mashat*), among others, yesterday.

•

Are states, made up of people, *things*?

•

She says I am adamantly non-linear. (Is that what she said?)

•

Think abroad.

•

Occasionally the mildness overwhelms: the air is so caressing, you can't help crying out.

•

I need to continue doing both and all.

•

I could use a crayon or two, something Crayola to mark the walls.

The possibility of a good, frightening judgment day: titillating.

•

I want to be everything but lazy.

•

Just finished my one daily shot. I write myself into a stupor, arousal, a continuing glance.

•

Is this a bruise—or a wound?

•

My friend, the weaver—no one would call weaving a sickness.

•

So I am—mortified?

•

She likened it to the host—Jesus bread. Each piece part of something larger and an entirety unto itself.

•

(Looks are deceptive: it has risen and been punched down multiple times.)

•

It begins like this: Now I lay me down to sleep.

And so I rob myself, along the way.

•

What did she say? The words themselves register as skin? Register on skin?

Skin is the thing.

•

Keeping myself company. (a lonely way to go)

•

Continuing the process of making nuggets. Rolling snow balls? Rubber band balls?

Can't figure out how to organize myself.

(Something with a little more skin to it?)

•

If I went to church, maybe I would be better at showing my emotions in public places?

•

I may dabble in many languages, but I still can't speak in my own tongue.

(In Hebrew and Greek, it's the same word for both.)

•

Nodes—the word I'm looking for:

•

As soon as I turn off the music, it's gone; I can't complete the emotion without the song.

•

Just ride out into some sunset or other

•

a thin narrative, getting thinner.

•

This isn't ending now; this won't end until it's over.

•

Talking to you again!

•

Like chocolate, she said. Meaning, I guess, that it's probably arbitrary.

•

savor/bask

•

We need to get back to our black selves, where sadness roars.

•

My mother said: You're my mother. Then, she said: I said something wrong, didn't I?

•

Highly unlikely that I'll ever learn Bulgarian.

•

It all resulted in a headache, though I'm not sure why. It may have been the wind.

•

Rumblings is the word she collected from last night's talk on Laplanche.

•

(You know what you need to do but can you make yourself do it?)

•

I have become expert at forgetting.

•

(If only I could report from another world—or place, at least.)

The teeth are bothering her tonight; she takes them out, puts them in a cup.

•

Rumblings: From the parental bedroom. From the earth (when it loses balance and quakes). From our throats, when emotion renders language inchoate.

•

How would you begin to talk about a good grief?

•

Without a padding of language, the world is too close.

Morning.

•

Started Arabic last night!

•

I send him outrageously arousing email, and can't desist.

•

Back in the saddle,

•

Didn't I once read that a fish hears all up and down its body?

•

(the usefulness of fasting, a finite version of starvation)

•

Suddenly, there's a lot to talk about.

•

The one problem I see? Giving you a name and calling you by it.

But then, like any deity, you go by many names. How am I supposed to keep them straight?

Isn't it simpler to address you by the force of my gaze?

•

My sister says that I'm too generous; I didn't know there was an alternative.

•

(I didn't leave a tip, but it turns out I was astonishingly open-handed.)

•

Haven't seen any animals today but yesterday I saw a squirrel.

•

Mirror facing a mirror: without end.

•

If I were an analyst's mother, I am the patient I would want for my analyst son or daughter.

But analysts arrive as adults, fully formed, directly from Freud's head.

•

There are children in the streets, children with parents. A child with a bag, something holy in the bag.

(About to be placed in the mouth—holiest of holies!)

•

As he spoke, I noticed that his lips were purple.

I can't say what he did or didn't understand; I suppose my point was that the saying, and what was said, was my prerogative.

•

He spotted me on the street and said my name.

•

In this city, birds have lost their fear: they swoop so close now, we feel the wind of them.

•

(Dreamt we kissed so hard that thin, white pieces of skin came away from my mouth.)

•

So much of what I listen for is contained in a kind of silence; I hear it only with this ancient ear running the length of my fish body.

•

The first months of this analysis, she stole my clock, my compass—oh, admit it!—she inhabited your bones.

•

I have a Barney's card and a Neiman Marcus card. I am growing up!

•

Left there crumpled like a coat that should've stayed home on a hanger.

•

Is it simply the nature of a sister to make you sometimes feel that she's too much everything?

•

People on the street passing each other with a keen regard. We almost passed each other by yesterday, but he stopped me.

The world turned incrementally on its axis, then we each went our way.

•

I think I've mostly gotten what I wanted from it: a solid erotic base.

•

My mother greets me from a chair, in a nightgown. Her once-beautiful legs are too thin now and marked.

For minutes she doesn't quite register where she is or that I'm there. She sees and then can't see. She focuses, when she can, and I am there for her.

It is the same for me: she is there and not there. She comes into focus and goes.

•

How can we keep doing this?

•

This is a fact.

You think about fucking it, you feel faint.

•

I could use any words, I think, as long as I endowed them with warmth and love—she turns toward me and basks.

Like a baby, but not. She understands that this isn't the way things should be.

•

I'm no longer capable of being the mother I was; I didn't even give my son a card on his birthday.

•

I write to him saying: My mother may have had a small stroke.

I delete the letter.

I write to him saying: I am weak with love for you.

•

He writes: You are ablaze, my love.

I write: Ablaze and weak, both.

I love you without end. (*bli sof, sans fini, horis telos, bitsiz*)

•

Went downtown for clothes and ended up with jewelry.

•

I want to take her face in my hands and say: What do you want me to do? What do you want me to know? I'm right here, Mom!

•

Need to follow the words to the place where meaning reverberates toward silence.

•

I miss his hands, his eyes, the things he said to me thirty-four years ago, his tongue, the roof of his mouth, his lips—his lips on my lips—these speaking lips and those, signing another language entirely, but still within the human realm, in fact, the perfect crossover.

•

Plenty comes with plenty. You give up the drought and the flood arrives—all ways.

•

My mother in a nightgown—white with small blue flowers. Her legs are white, with small blue flowers.

•

These new syllables require a new mouth. I've made mine more agile for him, more worldly. And still don't know how to tell him I love you in enough languages.

•

We changed a few mirrors in the house; we're aiming to look at ourselves differently.

•

Thirty years ago today, I pushed him out into the world with great heaves—and then he was here, red (a little blue), squawking! squalling! covered in something white.

•

I pointed my index fingers, jabbed them a little playfully into his chest. I own him, a little, after all.

•

I own the men? (Or the men own me?)

•

Ownership, money, banks, businesses. I, a business? More likely a ewe.

•

Time to get hopping.

•

I'm thinking about lingerie (her word), I'm thinking about (my legs in) sheer black stockings.

•

On paper, I've given her a name; that takes care of something.

Time to get going, time to pay attention.

•

My mother, in a white nightgown with small blue flowers, a cotton nightgown, her once-silky legs.

She looks at you like you're someone new—and then you are.

•

Father's Day. (no more fathers)

(the mothers, fast dwindling)

•

Sometimes when you're nervous, the only thing you can think of doing is something that will make you more nervous.

•

Odd compromises.

•

This is the thing: this she is real.

•

You have a mother and she's there for all time.

•

Where do you wear your skin? (Do you wear it or does it wear you?)

These days (no doubt about it), I'm worn.

•

One of the things I was desperate to tell you is this: We met a hero.

The hero said: Don't be naïve.

•

Her life wings her skyward.

(Remember: wax)

•

Pretend false endlessness?

•

I can say anything I can think (up); all I need to do is avoid the censorship of you.

•

Finish the story.

Read to the end.

•

Summer solstice.

Eat corn.

•

It's so easy to get caught on thin wires, stuck in corners, wrapped in transparent paper, a mess.

•

My calcium: Bone-Up.

•

So, what about heroes?

•

Sometimes you address yourself, sometimes you don't.

When you do, the you and the other—him, her, anyone—become submerged in your oceany self.

•

You tend to drown until you bob.

•

(a version of float)

•

Once, on a raft, a boy drew on your back—numbers that wouldn't stop. Maybe it was letters.

An unknown sequence, at any rate.

You must have been sweet: two boys came back later, as men, for more.

An examination of your store.

(The goods on your shelves.)

(What money can't buy.)

•

The light changed. We crossed.

•

Is this a crisis?

•

Our blockade?

•

(our sanctimoniousness)

•

Have we agreed to make a deal?

When are we closing?

(Everything I own in escrow; everything I am.)

•

Are any of my waters international?

•

(Will I still be here without you?)

•

I shopped for a new wardrobe, considering myself new.

•

Who can sleep more than four hours?

My husband's teeth.

Why is the song gone, just one day later?

•

I can stand my ground.

•

a tunnel economy

•

Everything you eat, covered in sand.

A constant beach (in your teeth).

•

Inhabited. There's no other way of talking about it.

I fling words at you.

•

Sometimes, all that's wanted is a listening ear.

It's become apparent: the style of your listening opposes my
desires.

•

Flung like so many plagues on the end of a fingertip.

Drops of wine (stain a white cloth)

•

I can stand my ground.

•

My lingerie has a place in this discussion.

•

Losing one's tools?

•

Why do YOU get to be the interviewer?

(the interrogator)

the interloper

•

Opals: small fires.

•

Don't speak to me, I'm concentrating.

Stop talking, I'm coming.

•

Where do you get your (drinking) water?

Where do you dig your well?

•

I crave his bones.

(I order steak.)

•

Who can paddle sand?

•

My mother hallucinates a me not me.

•

Walk into the house and hear long soprano trills.

The Alzheimer's soprano?

•

In the news: Israel relaxes Gaza blockade.

We are eased?

•

Expand the flow of goods!

Let them taste cinnamon and cardamom. Let them know their dead grandmothers in the spices.

•

You tunnel into me, throwing the sand of my bones, the liquid of my heart into a spare house at the top of the road.

No one knows it's there, or so you say.

I'm terrified.

Anyone may venture upon it, take the stuff of my stuff and start hauling it away.

•

I can't remember what day it is, what month we're in.

The weather is fine. Thin, graceful clouds, like fingers, a streak of tears.

Always putting a mother in the kitchen.

•

How do I find my way back to yesterday?

•

(It may not have been what you think.)

•

Socked in with fog.

•

I keep thinking to call my mother and tell her how life has been with me.

•

When those two came apart, the world sighed.

•

Why do tears always come on airplanes? Need to buy a handkerchief.

•

Sitting around in a Mormon town, not exactly incognito.

•

Jumping on a trampoline, fear jumps you high!

•

Panic twins with sadness, and lists Siamese. Only tears can pull them free.

•

A headache may require surrender, as well.

•

Anchored by sadness?

•

I wept into chlorinated water, winded by the altitude.

•

Planted in sadness, feet first.

•

She forms the cornerstone of my audience?

•

The point is to get it right: to both convey and portray adoration.

•

I can talk about what scares me, I can talk about beginnings.

•

How to back away from the present rapidly enough to see it true?

•

Pretty good at improvising in the atmosphere of my mind, but what about the air we all breathe?

•

A baby may calm you.

•

Public tears may overtake you.

•

I could use a little melting—this hot wax of me.

•

Here comes the harpist, wheeling it in!

•

My mother cocooned in the soft prison of herself.
Good night.

•

Waxing nostalgic isn't a sin.
Sometimes can't tell sadness from gratitude.

•

No she, no me.
But I do love the colors on this new purse.

•

Sometimes, at the end of the flight, at the end of the day—you are small and small only.

•

Fog—thank god.

•

Cutting it into more manageable bites.

•

We just coo at each other and make up odd bits of lullaby, nursery rhyme, old-age home rhyme.

•

Title: Emotional Vocalizing

•

I told her that the only words I had in my mind were: You've forsaken me.

She said: If you take apart the word, there's another message.

•

For (your) sake. Of course.

•

Time for a walk?

•

An impatient patient?

•

My mother declines heartily.

•

Everyone on a tether...

•

But something in me also says: This isn't really open to

discussion.

I left there furious and frustrated to tears.

•

Thinking about him, I nearly came. Just: here in a chair in a room lit by a lamp, pre-dawn.

•

My husband's temporary teeth fell apart in his mouth as he was swimming in the Aegean.

•

Here by the Bay, I watch my mother's life wind down.

•

Walking toward a place where words thin out, lose sense.

•

watching her fade

•

I quietly closed a door on that friend.

•

She maintains an atmosphere friendly to ambiguity—I guess that's her job.

•

(Everything's ambiguous, until it's not.)

•

My sister and I contemplate telling them to stop pushing the Ensure. Would that be something like murder?

•

No longer afraid of rogue terrorists.

•

Trying not to talk to her, preparing for the future.

But I can't stop imagining an ear: it's been there my whole life.

•

entirely dependent on the chemical wash of blood and caffeine

I can come out fighting.

•

wildly sad

So this is it. I guess I'm ready.

•

The drama of a life, my mother's, being played out each day. And then it will subside—and only be carried on within the rest of us.

•

Hospital bed on its way, and morphine.

Fog.

•

I can't go beyond the gurgles and sounds that occur inside me.

•

Terrified, unquiet.

She knows she's dying.

•

Who are you arguing with? she asked.

•

Talking truth with my sister. Talking truth to truth, rejecting inanity and every distraction.

•

Fog, the feel of the air, the attempt to know what you're walking through, the tilt of the earth, the rumble of the sea.

My mother and my mother, only.

Trying to tell her: I *know* you.

•

Ate a burger. Broccolini.

•

I walk that hill, aiming for the peak. Sometimes it comes too quickly.

•

These skateboarders go past at any time, awakening us from fleet dreams.

•

Keep doing this?

•

I thought: Okay, I can still call my husband.

Forgetting that we'd just hung up.

Misery.

•

She said: You mean that coming here makes you feel worse?

•

I ask her: Do you want a burger, Mom? Do you want to go to a movie and then dinner? She considers, then says: Maybe.

Laughing, a person gives up fear—even if only for a second.

•

Maybe the simplest thing to say is this: Like a prophet, you were waiting for the moment when you could utter those words.

•

Some air was finally let out today. I, a balloon. (spinning out into the atmosphere until its air will have depleted)

•

In order to be able to take my husband's cock in my mouth, my mother will first have to die.

This is not the kind of daughter I am, it's just the way it goes.

•

Mostly freezing.

•

Today, she seemed to have gone through some huge trial: her eyes were so sad.

But I guess that was me.

•

Solace in the familiar yet still exotic syllables of Hebrew.

•

It didn't open up, exactly, but it was suddenly, fully there.

•

I keep buying leather.

•

I told her: This is not something I can't take.

•

My friend gave me ice cream for my birthday.

•

Fog again.

•

Garbage day! I hear them coming!

Am I happy, or what?

My mother is dying.

(That's not what I meant.)

•

Sometimes, leaving your house, you need a skin in addition to the one you can't help wearing.

•

I didn't—until now.

•

She said: Your voice was more forceful, a little angry, the other day.

I asked: Are you criticizing me?

•

She asked: But what's going to happen?

She said: My body.

•

No longer in Israel, that's for sure.

•

Full adult or half?

•

She has many names, including the absence of one.

•

I caught a glimpse of one perfect white hip today.

•

The mother is on her way out. We could use an inrush of fathers.

•

Trying to be here and here at once. No go.

•

I began wearing glasses in order to read the tiny vowels in Arabic.

•

Sadness is across the separation wall.

•

If the food is let go, so will the woman.

•

Her bed, a remnant of womb.

•

I can't seem to separate from this cashmere sweater; I can't take it off.

•

In bed this morning: Oh, please, just be nice to yourself. *Please!*

•

Fur or skin—that's the question.

•

(Only a letter's difference between adore and adorn.)

•

Need to wear something warmer.

It's almost snowing in here.

•

She isn't eating anymore. We are letting her go.

•

Skin or hair? Fur?

•

This cold—as if I were the one dying, not her.

•

Does a child grow to ever want anyone more than it wanted its mother?

•

blanket, web, teether (tether)

•

as if I would accompany her to the grave

•

terribly inadequate

•

I wear cashmere and will never take it off.

(except, perhaps, for leather)

•

I said: My attitude right now? Fuck words.

She said: I thought there was a fuck in there somewhere—and I don't mean a sexual one.

I said: Oh, that's in there, too.

I couldn't help smiling.

There's nothing I can't be cajoled out of.

•

She used "ice cream" to fill in her own blanks today; we laughed.

•

Saw her naked body, where I had my start. There's nothing ugly about her, even now. Her body is perfect and perfectly cared for, her skin hardly wrinkled.

•

I found what I can do: I hold her hands.

The flesh of others is only as solid or pure as your own.

•

She quoted Winnicott: An analyst needs to stay awake, alive, and well.

Like anyone, right?

•

Richness arrives; I've simply been waiting for her to die.

•

It could start: Fuck words.

•

(I can hardly write that word, "Mom"—it looks like her face.)

•

It and I, my writing and my self, are entwined in new, fascinating ways.

•

A raft set up before the ship was due to wreck, before the people almost drowned.

•

Walking these streets, eating strawberries, pouring water, driving, listening to the radio, opening the fridge.

•

Pubic bone not at all bare, and more where it's needed, at the lips. That's my mother. Other writers have used the word porcelain for thighs. Hers aren't that—they give—but they're white and without blemish.

•

My husband just came up on my screen. Entered me.

•

Time snapped to, connected to the previous length of it: I'm at my mother's deathbed.

•

I'm watching the slow motions of death: my mother's wiles—the screams that seem precautionary rather than a direct response to pain—and death's, a smutty mistress.

•

What Hebrew does now, in my time of need?

•

I find a hand inside my bra, squeezing a nipple.

•

She misunderstood the doctor's instructions—yesterday, she sort of overdosed my mother, who went through the day calm as a corpse.

She admits her mistake, and we laugh.

•

I think the word "fuck," which hadn't been said in that room, did a lot of work for us.

•

Hands offer themselves to each other.

•

Hebrew woos me, soothes me; I can hear the Arabic inside it.

•

My mother's mouth, slack with a little thickened saliva visible. Yesterday, her left eye kept tearing. I asked: Mom, are you crying?

•

Her eyes are still there but faint and drifty, looking up, fixed on something none of us can see.

•

In my mother's battles, there are good guys and bad. Sometimes she's on one side, sometimes the other. Her screams are loud!

•

Yesterday, I had to ask: And if I administer the morphine and she dies, no one's going to take me to jail, right?

They said: Morphine doesn't kill; starvation doesn't hurt.

•

I could collect things. I could make a life of collectibles.

•

(Words, collated in text: a face.)

•

We're having a party: celebrating her life, her spawn, in the big yellow bedroom, with the hospital bed, all her girls together on one wide chair.

•

Our mother, unable to hold herself up, leans against the side of the commode, babbles words, syllables, bits of her life, her personality sputtering to an end in the yellow room lit north and south through French doors with their view of tousled magnolia leaves.

She doesn't know where or what she is, her body flung here and there.

•

I've become used to the comment her sparse pubis seems to make. Not angry, but still there.

•

We go crazy right here, listening to loud music, dancing our shoulders around, bouncing on the balls of our feet.

•

Outside the walls—birdsong, quiet green leaves.

She keeps trying to figure it out: Where am I?

(Halfway there?)

•

Just ordered burgers, chicken, fries, salad, broccolini. Chocolate-peanut-butter ice cream.

People have to eat.

•

speaking, singing, incanting as I type

•

Maybe you want to know what "in the thick of it" really means.

•

Watching her go, we touch her hands, her face, kiss her forehead and cheeks, touch her chin, not quite touching her.

•

Divergent thoughts? Convergent?

•

Is it the lack of sleep that makes times exciting or exciting times that make you lose sleep?

•

Those little tops I've cut off the strawberries, a bit of leaf and the pocked red skin.

•

I can hardly eat.

•

And find myself staring (tired), the way she does.

•

Losing my appetite.

•

We went through the house, the two of us, and realized how small a life is.

•

My body sings a little wasting away song every time it thinks of him.

•

We walked through the house, container of a life—bowl, platter, cup, sieve—Goodbye!

•

These things she chose and loved, these things she touched and breathed. Bathtub, toilet seat, sink. Hairbrush, lipstick, soap. Perfume—twirling the air of her.

•

Fog and the plum trees, bucking as usual.

Nipples erect. Still waiting.

•

I write (my way) through this day, which is to say

•

That young black man on the street, nodding at me through his headphones, just like that, human. It's what tends to make me cry.

•

A wide length of geography: a line of longitude, a swing to rest on, something—amen—to see us through. A destination, a curve of atmosphere to slump against in the possible later.

•

(another kind of every which way)

•

I've been barking up the wrong tree: it's a song, you make it up as you go along.

•

Someday, baby, I'm going to have to say: Look at everything showing between the dollars, everything not measured or measurable, your supple boundaries, leaping, occasionally, by bounds, across the plain of me, wildflower, grass, mud, ant, gnat, dung. Sung, every bit of it, with our tongues.

•

Rebirth?

•

It goes anywhere, won't be turned away, seeks cracks, flattens thin, sparks fire, wreaks havoc, shows up on the other side.

•

Just talked to my husband. In the silence that arose after fifteen minutes of chatter, my body took over—I had to lean against a wall.

•

What I've been trying to say: raft, safety net, parachute.

(sturdy shoes, protein bar, canteen)

•

These threes: parents and a child.

•

Her life—we open our hands to catch it—gone.

Dandelion fluff. A puff. One breath and she's gone.

•

With no husband to yank me to the earth, I admit, I'm always flying around. This spacious body knows no ups or downs without him.

(Salad tossed in its own dressing.)

•

I finished my early morning bowl of quinoa, one word in my mouth: *bochim*. We are crying.

•

My mother's eyes go skyward. Watching? Waiting?

The things she says: Are you ready? How will we get there?

•

Small cut-up sounds escape her mouth, nothing whole or definite—and then it's there, out of the blue, her regular voice.

•

Wearing cashmere, soft like a mother.

•

Flight, but with our toes still touching the ground.

•

Each day seems like two or more. I am awake at four or five. I lie in the dark until I can't.

•

Smoothed my mother's hair for a long time; I held her hands.

•

Breathed motionlessness into my mother last night, no other prayer.

•

She was more coherent last night than she had been in days; it was almost a regular conversation.

•

Dying is torture, with periods of calm.

Like birthing a baby.

·

I wake up in the night, frozen to my bed by a thought.

·

In the end, you need someone to help you repeat the names of those you love.

She repeats the names like hands, like handholds.

·

If I were you, this time in a patient's life would be my favorite.

·

They wash her head to toe, beginning with the most intimate parts, then her belly, back, arms, neck, then face, and at the end, her legs and feet, each toe and in between. They put powder under her breasts and lotion everywhere else.

For years, she didn't want them to touch her. Now, when they do, she purrs.

Like a cat, her eyes just slits.

·

We want to know who gets what and how the division will take place.

(We're dying to know who we will be when the dying gets done.)

·

I look at her as they bathe her, the perfect line of leg and hip. Her shins are a little banged up, a little ugly, but there are no other ugly parts to my mother. She sports a fluff of pubic hair, not sparse at all. With her clothes off, my mother looks larger than she did for so long. Ample hips, belly, thighs. She's hardly wrinkled, just dry until they rub in lotion.

Those moles beneath her breasts—I didn't know about them. Two scars, one up her back, one diagonal on her belly. Her ass is what it's always been—a little flat.

•

My mother's face turns multicolored in an instant. What I'm learning? Dying is agony. Those screams she forces out. Giving birth? (to death) The people in the house next door

She wants her daughters near. I'll have no daughters to stare at my fluffy pussy on my deathbed and think: that's where I entered the world.

Birth screams, a bit torn.

•

Simple white shroud. Poplar (unfinished) coffin. *Shomer* to see her through the night. Viewing, optional.

•

I remembered to bring a protein bar but forgot my toothbrush. My mother screamed her way through the day.

We've begun to cry.

•

Her features twisting monstrous.

•

My mother, the house of her, breaking down, caving in.

Today, she raised her legs as if she was giving birth, and screamed and heaved, trying to push something out.

What is a mother but a house? This one has been so solid, even in illness and bad weather, dependable.

We've always had a mother.

•

My analyst is kind. Today, she wore something blue to keep away the evil eye.

•

At the head of this bed—a sea of pictures. A lot of old me's.

•

Quiet. Night comes in, but gently.

•

My sister and I say: blank.

•

This unassuming house with its inward and invisible charms, its surprising beauties, its breath of fresh air, its trees, right at the center of it. Out of view of strangers. It sits on a street with other, far grander houses. It holds its own.

•

That poor woman at the funeral home. How we torture her!

•

When you get to the real thing, there's no place or need for irony. Sarcasm exits the room.

•

This house, this house of her.

I concentrate, falling into a weightiness that doesn't admit much thought.

This house in the sun, bathed in light.

Hydrangeas on the wall and in a vase. These pieces of wood, wool, cotton. Shaped and

•

Her breath—shallow.

•

I hold this flat round bear; I stare at the lips of my mother's vagina.

I stare, the pubic hair—too numerous and still-wild to count. Wild! She's going out wild, though right now, at noon on a Wednesday, she's quiet, folded onto her left side, my sister leaning toward her, just above the white blanket that's taken the shape of her body.

She is still alive.

Hydrangeas in a vase with water (but dying) and on the wall—all the way from China?

•

As long as it's the right people, there's nothing better than people.

•

I gave my sister instructions: You can always win me back by saying you love me.

•

Ate those licorice pastels that have been in a plastic jar in the kitchen for years. But they didn't taste old.

•

Out of the box of me, into the house of you.

•

Less rigid than bone, harder than water.

•

I love the idea of God, but don't believe in it. Even today.

•

My mother's eyes are open, she blinks, she breathes—smoothly, for the most part.

Night time, at last.

•

Swam today. I keep trying. She keeps living. We're tired.

•

Brain works in the beginning of the day, but not so well later on.

•

We're full of sweet nothings, whispered in her ears, blown against her face, kisses. I kiss her many times, unable to pull away. I stare at her face and fall into silence.

•

Religion starts in the death of a parent?

•

First morphine of the day, 10:30 a.m.

Quiet over here, foggy.

She calls me. I think she's calling me. Still here. Her knuckles are a little blue today. Her face a little sallow. Lips still red.

•

Something in me feels on the verge of gagging.

•

Talking together on the phone, he gets hard; I get wet.

•

My mother is drowning in her own fluid and I'm eating tortillas with peanut butter.

•

My sister said: What do you need? You need earrings, don't you?

•

She never learned to swim and now she's drowning to death, surrounded by air, in her own home.

•

I guess now I can say that I know what a death rattle sounds like.

•

The phone keeps ringing.

Her face is grey now with little dabs of rosiness.

The sky has changed—clouds and a little wind. The window is open but maybe it shouldn't be.

•

My mother and I, my mother and I, my mother.

•

Sisters sitting in the sun together, some far-off afternoon in a place

•

Her breathing is quieter.

•

The sky has gone blue again, no clouds.

•

I'm in love with the Arabic word *dakika* (same in Hebrew), "minute," the way it sounds, what it means, the way it's written:

دقيقة

A written mantra.

Things here are not morose.

•

Dying is so sexual. I watched my mother do it.

•

I went and found him under the covers, devoured him and, a bit like my mother in her last hours, couldn't control the sounds that issued from me.

•

Receding? Or coming clear?

•

My analyst called the house the night my mother died and my husband thought she was selling something.

Sanity!

•

I can still write. (My mother is dead. My little mother.)

•

Pictures?

I could have (should have?

Too late now) taken more.

•

A fine nurse helped bring her back so that she could die simply by taking small and smaller sips of breath until there were no more sips to take. Stubborn surrender.

•

My niece says: My mom shops when she's sad.

My nephew says: She shops when she's happy, too!

•

When the hearse arrived, I ran to it.

•

"The piece of my heart where your name is written will be the last to go."

•

I have above-the-knee boots.

•

Sacred: I couldn't say my therapist's name to her face until the morning of the day my mother died.

She offered mine back to me.

•

Salami for breakfast. Something in me can't get enough—salt?

•

I melt at his touch but am generally mean.

•

So eager for those brussels sprouts last night that I burnt the hell out of my mouth.

•

There is writing that's like a bad fuck, and writing that's like a fucking dream.

•

Hands: I sit on them to quiet their flight.

•

My mother's eyebrows needed plucking, but it was a little late.

•

I have to assume that if the room seems like itself again, maybe I do, as well.

•

Thursday: touched her coffin and cried.

•

I am singing again. Singing, I am fine.

•

Screamed at my husband this morning; he's always talking to me.

•

A team of window-washers came and made ours see-through. Walk through what appears invisible, straight to the other side?

•

Pulled on my not-short hair but none of it came out.

•

That tiny puff of air my mother kept quacking out and tonguing in—is that all any of us ever have?

•

Let's hope it turns out to be a good surprise.

•

That infinitesimal breath my mother kept recycling, the being of her refusing to go out, refusing to be quenched.

•

I've forgotten how to hum? To sing a hymn? To be a tree but the kind of tree that can open its legs?

•

Let's not sew it up tonight; let's keep this wound open, suppurating.

•

Sometimes, everything is gone.

•

A bit frigid, a bit unable to come. Until I did.

This, a long kaddish?

He fucked me every which way, a seventy-year-old acting like a teenager.

•

Either a monster of health or vaguely sick?

•

I love being able to look at him across space, then bridge it with steps.

•

A constant tightrope walk, she said.

•

Desire, impossible to manipulate, is what I desire.

Hungry. Oh well.

•

A love affair, a smattering of inky shapes. Something cruising that can't be made to stop.

•

A belief in beginnings, and *omphaloi*. Points of connection, points of no return.

His penis, my mouth, his fingers, mine, an asshole (or two)—the star of it—my throat, my tongue, his. Mine. My cunt, an angel. Pinched nipples, *pinched*.

•

I haven't: read or studied languages in ages.

•

Worked out, bought books and five pounds of English peas.

Someone from the Giants just hit a grand slam in the bottom of the tenth inning.

I went to my mother's house and took out the garbage cans. Peed (marking territory?). Looked around at the house in the light.

•

All those buttons a person collects from shirts and sweaters.

•

Something came back to life today; some fog lifted.

•

Your heart, my lung.

Those days, infused

•

(her) beautiful hands

•

Tomorrow, Arabic!

Next week, Spanish!

•

Nothing else, just.

•

Passing people on streets is remarkably therapeutic.

•

I will walk in tomorrow at seven, a picture of perfect (mental) health.

•

My mother's house, so obviously a womb, now a tomb.

I go there alone, mingle with ghosts.

•

Can't help suspecting the everything of me.

•

I can go to the gym, I can jump in the pool.

•

Need to write something or edit something.

•

I've still not filled her hands with tears.

•

Trying to preserve myself—jam?

•

Is she trying to fix me mad?

•

Arabic jolted me

•

Ready to fall on my knees, press my face to the ground—rug, sidewalk, earth—kiss it, lick it, smear it with tears.

•

My husband (not a project, something to be savored, a long meal)

•

I miss the constant ping of that long fling

•

Something like a blue moon? Or a particular configuration of the sun, moon, and earth?

•

Sad, furious, scared. What a combination.

•

New month.

•

adamantly, insistently, deliciously secular

•

The decision was unspoken and unanimous: empty and sell it as quickly as possible.

•

Thick fog.

•

I can and then I can't and then I can again.

•

Brilliant constellation or richly idiotic?

Snap peas. Organic lettuce.

Our tongues, dueling (playfully).

-

Heroes: speak truth to the status quo.

-

I collect simultaneous translators as trinkets because I can't be one myself.

-

That quality of velocity. One can't be "aloft" without great speed.

Not concerned with life after death but with everything up until.

-

(The legitimacy of a mode called "ache"?)

-

Located in the atmosphere, eros, a different logic holds sway.

You bite into anything that looks juicy.

-

Prodding the physical, do I touch touch?

(only you can say)

-

Here in the erotic: your glance, my tongue.

-

I may someday have to go back to writing something more conventional but until I do, I won't.

Something Slavic?

-

between my legs and reading

•

The rabbi intoned prayers in both the known language and
the familial, ancient one. The sun shone. A helicopter passed
overhead. We had watched her retire from life, not easily, three
days before. Strong men raised her onto a shelf, sealed her in with
glue. Her husband, the humus of him, above.

•

Trying not to be a berserker bear.

One must live and write at the (exact) same moment.

•

Something about time just became so sweet I could call it
"darling." Imagine, time itself, that just took my mother from me!

A favorite dictator?

I heil this Hitler, sun and moon looking on.

•

Feeling well and well.

Attaining velocity.

Once again, taking off.

(dearest)

•

Life turns and turns.

He's cooking something the scent of which drives me toward him.

•

A mother, indistinguishable from a house.

Capacious, even when small.

•

Yitgadal v'yitkadash

•

One declares one's health on faith.

•

Burning up and coming to.

•

A mind to navigate time.

•

Everything is fodder, anything may turn out to be something.

•

I can say anything on paper.

I can almost touch you.

(any part of you)

•

My mother hasn't come back—I should have known.

•

Where do you find space? Assuming that what you want is (empty).

•

Me and my wilds.

•

The night my mother died, I went berserk until I touched his body. Then, the mingling of his things with mine took another form, no mess, all beauty and grace. We were acrobatic, in perfect tension, incapable of quieting ourselves.

•

You think grief will take you away from yourself, but it just gives you more. That's the scary part, how much you there may actually be.

•

The very small thing happened on the day after my 51st birthday: a good man had a confused moment and put a finger where he shouldn't have, then a year and twelve days later, my mother died.

When I saw the man on the street a month before her death, he apologized to me. I pointed both index fingers at his chest, leaned in, touching him, and said: You know what? I turned it gift.

•

This grief, this mourning is not what they tell you it will be.

•

Her last taste, aside from morphine, was vanilla Ensure. She purred with the tastiness of it. We purred along, we hummed.

•

Tomorrow, it will have been three weeks: we're still thick as thieves.

I dream awake, I sleep upright.

LOVE LETTERS

You ordain the fickleness of me: a couplet.

•

Pushed toward a different hesitation, clad in syllables?

•

It's about letting the mind spin; this may be where you came in.

•

Good things come raining down; I open out—an umbrella.

•

The being of us opened, made rain!

That's a god, isn't it?

•

Sometimes he soaks me, sometimes the mist of you

•

Oh, making love to an audience.

It comes naturally to you, he said.

•

Fall is here, almost crisp. That dog's ears touched the leaves, swept them around.

•

I can be solemn or less solemn.

•

My mother is gone, her house has been sold.

I put myself in the garment of her, weep into a pocket.

•

Am now returned to you on this borrowed book of time.

You—also a library?

A full self requires stillness.

I am coming upon the face, the shape of it.

•

Scratched pots and pans, wooden mallets hard enough to beat in a head. Sieves, bowls, scissors, tongs. Ladles.

Have we humiliated the house of our mother?

•

Saw both sons within a twenty-four hour period.

The accompanying sound: a kind of purr.

•

"...Winnicott postulates the existence of a psychological intermediary realm between the subjective and the objective that he calls transitional space."

Here we are.

•

I was furious with him for making it so hard but the truth is that I hadn't done my homework.

•

I said: I'm just about done with my mother's house.

She said: You're never done with your mother's house.

•

I could say to her: Are you saying that my work is anorexic?

•

I sat in a kind of calm confusion, choosing not to define or decide.

•

No answers. I just want a good sex life.

•

What may feel like a tumble through space ends up feeling like a
fall.

•

No she in focus; no me.

•

Before, talking about sex made it present.

Now, talking confines it to deep pockets?

•

We're giving her away now, this time voluntarily.

The things arrayed.

The bulk and heft of her.

•

Working on the piece. This piece of the piece.

•

Rape? Or the unclothing of a life?

so much dust

That (Trojan?) horse of a piano on its side, blanketed, cossetted.

chests and bowls—holders, like a mother

Leaves in the entranceway. A running faucet. Doors banging open
and shut with the wind.

Raped? Abandoned.

•

Now, she said, you've got me.

Then, she corrected herself: We've got each other.

I had no words.

•

Everything in here seems momentous.

Like an earthquake?

That's when it hit.

•

I can only make things taut; I have no interest in roundabout or loose.

•

This drawn-out shiva.

Sitting, we keep each other company.

•

Dream: She couldn't have died if the person before her in line was still alive.

•

That woman (in me) who goes to midnight Mass in order to brush against other human beings—

I can't not love her.

•

One skin gone, the other arrives.

•

Occasionally, she holds her own hand.

(Occasionally, she stabs herself with whatever is at hand, sharp or dull.)

•

your address, my erotic life

•

I've shut the door on that friendship.

Another abdication? How many abdications in a year?

•

Mustard greens and curly kale with string beans and boiled
potatoes. Hot, in the pot.

•

I may go in there and say: I think I've stumbled upon our
mortality.

•

These frequent, cheap snorts of dream.

•

When I finished that piece, I wanted to know what was for
breakfast.

•

Mortality may jump on the bandwagon, mortality may ruin your
plans.

•

I want to ask her simple things: Do you like olives?

•

A relationship begun in an abundance of syllables, some remain
unpronounceable.

•

A mutual glance sparks recognition:

I know you, my self.

•

The scent of our time, atomized.

Who owns that scent?

•

The trick, I guess, is in knowing where to put up fences, how to tie off boundaries.

•

my muse, my air, a valence, my permission slip

•

"How we imagine property is how we imagine ourselves." (Hyde)

Is that why I leave the door on the latch whenever I go for a walk?

•

This bowl filling up with fragments of meditated time and image—

almost a wailing wall.

•

She said canticle and I said: If not kaddish, then simple prayer.

•

What I cry about?

My son on stage, forgetting he's my son.

•

It sings in me, you're right.

He sings, as well.

•

What do you call the commons of a brain? Isn't everything your birthright?

•

Begin (your parable, your legend) on a day when home is not a prison, when home is a commons, a field, a harvest about to begin.

How do you treat your commons?

And how do we negotiate the commons of our hours together—each one itemized, tallied, (paid for).

•

Sometimes I think we need to eat something together, a slice of baloney, a crust of bread, an olive, a pear, a peach.

We have drunk together, a sip, and a sip.

•

the extraction of grammar, a photosynthesis?

•

He has the voice, sings the song.

I make up the song, singing as I go along.

•

To go for the jugular: just another way of talking about a harvest?

•

I put you at the grocery store, watching me, then think of better places for you to be.

•

hoarder of space and time: objects of the mind

•

Flooded with refracted light off the water of a mother—she floats on timeless seas.

•

I face her, a you, and can't deny the truth of endings.

•

Look across and recognize this creak in the scenery.

A tear, a crack, the tears assemble, run down my face.

I wouldn't be surprised if they ran down yours as well.

•

This feels like tender new skin.

Tenderness may be inviting; people may respond in kind.

•

You find your old self, unabashed.

•

Turned off the greens. They'll continue to cook in their own heat, the boil of their being, the way things do.

•

The central molten boiling part: hardly an achievement, simply a fact.

•

My neck is getting old. It's true.

•

The grocery store *is* the place where one would fall on the floor, weeping, isn't it?

All those mothers.

•

When she makes gestures pointing to the fact that we commonly inhabit the world, I am moved to silence.

Is there a word for it?

Mortality?

•

She said: We haven't turned away from it at all.

•

I thought: Oh, this is life. I can still do this.

•

Anything that reeks of ripeness slays me.

•

In art, anything goes; it's not life.

•

Isn't sex everything? Oh, and nothing, too, I guess.

•

I said: I HATE not saying your name!

Then said it.

She said mine back.

•

9/11

(a date to make you stand up?)

•

Ate almonds and a protein bar, looked at expensive handbags online and now I'm calm?

•

Talking to my oldest friend on the phone today, for just under forty minutes, was like being at a fascinating cocktail party.

Sometimes, the world comes back to you, thank god.

•

Mondays are so reassuring.

•

an insane asylum: not exactly the Ritz

•

When I once said: We may be in it together, but you don't suffer.

She said: That's because I'm Irish and you're Jewish.

•

I cry, waking up and going to sleep.

•

Clarity is gone; I am here.

•

She is not my mother.

(You are not my mother.)

•

Confidence is not my forte?

•

I won't ever scream at him again for not closing the cupboards or for leaving his shoes in a mess.

•

You have been my everything—and now it's time to say goodbye?

•

Made it to here!

•

I keep remembering—before and after.

This after seems huge, the before irreplaceable and fragile.

•

A blossoming headache for days now—a kind of beauty, I guess.

•

Is that orchid with its four huge white blooms, almost insanely robust, me?

Is the dead-seeming one a remnant of my graceful, delicate mother?

She was never purple, but she could seem a little hothouse from time to time.

•

Measuring spoons, cup, thermometer. Hats and belts, sheets and towels. Buttons and thread. Shoes.

•

Where is your mother-in-law when you need her?

•

Here in a chair, surrounded by the elements: words, caffeine, sunlight, shadow.

•

That diabolical merry-go-round has spun itself out.

•

My friend and I walked the hill, touched the muzzles of frantic puppies.

•

My sister hates it when people tell her they're premenstrual.

But we're animal, after all.

•

I can't think that way—from one thing to the obvious next.

There's nothing quite so boring, unless you're trying to convince your husband of something.

•

Full moon.

•

Warming in a kind of afterlife, this life a little stolen from hers.

A bit finagled, like our precious time on earth.

•

The sun: orange and round, about to turn red, about to be elsewhere, as we are—together and apart.

•

Just us here now.

Hello! In every language.

•

A girl sings a self in the incantation of a mother.

•

professionally impressionable

•

You've eaten me with a spoon, cut through me with a sharp knife.

•

The sea rushes at this shore, this infinitely captive, captivating moment. She rushes, and we

•

It's the crest of the wave that dazzles, the astonishment of white.

A white we can't conceive without the knowledge of crashing waves.

•

I adore small, potent things.

•

Smaller than a bean, a pea: you pine for your mother.

•

Something happened: everything that had been simmering boiled over.

•

The quality of your attention drives me mad with grief.

Still, I can think of New York.

•

My husband waits, hovers, pretends to stomp away, pounces.

•

What, after all?

•

What method for handing you the hot wax of me?

For taking your impression onto me and making it last?

•

No atheist in the trenches: I'll keep resuscitating this love.

•

I've hardly slept. It's close to three. I'm ready to go.

Are you?

•

But sex often takes the rap.

•

Something in me can hardly think of her without keening.

She said: You were waiting for sadness; now you've got it.

•

But if I said I love you, would I be saying it as a woman or as a girl?

•

They always said: After this is over, we'll remember her when...

But I remember her then, right at the end. It's the her still closest to me.

•

How to put a coda on something never-ending?

●

Accumulate, abominate.

●

Oh, you mean the history of my sexuality!

This many years later, that fire still burns.

●

After buying the handbag in an air-conditioned store on a mostly empty downtown street, I drove Pine to the Pacific and who should I see from the corner of my eye but the undertaker. Driving the hearse, lighting a cigarette. I would know that man anywhere, with his blond hair and his dark, crazed look.

He lit up then moved lanes quickly, two over. I watched his left signal blinking red—I knew where he was headed.

The day after Halloween: splashed egg whites with a little shell mixed in. Red wax, chewed and spat. Dum Dum lollipops smashed, still in the wrapper.

•

All I know: no dodging emotion.

•

Each day, some letting of tears.

•

Often naked in my dreams these days.

•

Pitifully snide, small-minded, puny-hearted.

•

Ghosts?

•

Sometimes, old dreams come back.

In daylight, they're less startling.

•

This isn't stagnation—this is full speed ahead.

•

(Who is looking over my shoulder?)

•

If you don't face at least a sliver of it daily, it erupts.

•

My children?

•

(He was there to catch the nectar as it fell.)

•

Sometimes one's thumbs are so reminiscent of drumsticks.

•

Foghorns—finally.

•

I need to give up every last vestige of a mother?

•

On the plane. A little devastated.

•

I went to her with a handful of knots;

now, I hold all the strings?

•

like a bombed-out city

•

What I'm worried about? Life ever after.

•

One man said: I know this is a silly question, but: what is it to you?

What is breath?

•

Let that other thing go, is what I think. Not go go, but give it a rest.

•

Pecked at, glimpsed, (ogled, gnawed on). I put myself on display.

•

That was the autumn hotels lost their magic?

•

What is a bell's reverberation? Wave.

•

Our first day back, she removed her shoes, curled her feet beneath her and listened.

•

Looking for reasons, aiming for meaning.

•

You turn time over, fold it back and creep around in the underbrush.

•

This clot in my throat is a body's defense: grenade, calling card, abandoned mirror.

•

Is dislocation a form of prophecy?

Or just a slant?

•

We spoke of the illicit, dancing a memory.

I hold my own breast—needy.

•

9 a.m. Perfect blue skies

•

My table is clean, my ears are, too.

•

Los Angeles, where I am ready to be a little sexually aggressive with him.

•

Each session a small work of art.

•

His touch slows the world, speeds me up.

•

Do you really think that's likely?

Apparently not.

•

My cough: mostly wet but occasionally dry.

•

A hard day. But the work is ahead.

•

The jewelry has been divided: some for you and some for me.

•

I keep wishing I were myself as I was before. Healthy! Strong! Optimistic! Bombastic!

•

People pay attention: I say the things they're almost thinking.

•

Bronchial distress. I need to breathe!

•

Home—a miracle!

•

A sow's clitoris is inside her vagina.

Lucky girl!

•

Unpacked in less than half an hour.

•

I came out of that crying jag at dawn, looking out on palm trees.

•

This womb, responsive.

•

A beam of light skewers my tea, jiggles on the wall opposite me.

•

Still coughing, but trying to stand up straight.

•

She told me about the tear glass.

The nuns told the children—she was a small child, then—that when it fills, you die.

Lately, mine is filling up.

Half-empty?

•

Such a fat sack of brewing things:

I would steal the mother out from under her with the intensity of my need.

•

I think of my rocky village, I think of it now.

•

She said: And then you went back to sleep.

I said: Well, not exactly. By then, it was dawn.

She said: Oh, so it really was all night long.

•

What is it with this gold chain holding my mother's ring against my neck?

When does it tangle?

What causes it to knot?

•

(And when this thing is not right, no thing is.)

•

I will say: There are such competing accents in her speech!

•

Sick of my publicist; enamored of my audience.

•

Watch out! Your tear glass is dripping! It's running over!

•

She said: You know I'll be thinking of you.

You know I'll always be thinking of you.

I'll have you in mind.

I'll keep you in my mind.

I don't remember what she said but that's the gist.

•

Turning ungovernable; fear grows desire.

•

Even candy makes me cry—no longer mine. (That surrogate pleasure died with her.)

•

Like one piece of wood against another,

I spark myself against this page.

•

against you

•

(any you)

•

We seek peaks; they find us.

•

Stopped—almost. Stuck—in time.

Amber?

•

Need a shower to wash away the days.

•

Tears fell off the sides of my face; sadness may be a kind of bliss.

•

Need to walk toward fascination, peek at it, then pounce.

•

How do you divide humanity?

Haves and have-nots.

(But there are so many ways of having, a plethora of ways to have-not.)

•

These hours: incantatory.

•

What about these children of ours: watching us touch, being made to stare at us, touching?

•

Poetry?

Debunks the pretensions of a solid.

(Or: leads with the ear.)

•

The gifts of these last months: cigars.

Light one, inhale, blow smoke toward the fast-moving clouds.

•

The way people look to her now that she's dabbled in fame.

She fluctuates—all possibility; she's a slippery fish.

•

What are you going to do for an encore?

•

A mother is the ocean.

She takes everything and making liquid of it, pours it back toward you.

With a mother like that, you can give away endlessly, certain that everything will be returned.

•

People without children, without babies.

People tracing tightropes in their clogs.

Some characters we don't even purport to know.

•

All my concoctions too obvious? (too tame?)

•

You open it wider and wider—a cat's cradle between ten fingers— trying to see what you can see.

•

When my friends stop talking about me, I lose interest.

You? I would be overjoyed to know what you ate for lunch.

(You're neat: no crumbs.)

•

She sat with her volume of poems. Like a student, a school girl, a quiet mother, she gave birth to a world inside herself.

•

All over the map!

Truth AND consequences!

•

Paid my dues—to the ego of me, to the honesty and professionalism—the discreet wall of her.

•

The upshot?

It pours.

•

Trying to understand the balance of that scale: inside to outside.

•

This dark weather, apt.

•

Things have been burnished on the metal, embroidered on the sturdy cloth of me.

•

My mother raised girls, held a hand in each of hers—held on.

•

Rain today—relief.

•

I told her: solid, gas, liquid.

Her eyes lit up.

Aiming for an explanation in density.

•

Proud of our sanity.

(sometimes an effort, sometimes a breeze)

•

Sheep's wool: You card it to separate the fibers.

In one state of carding or another until I spin.

•

I don't even like eating candy anymore.

•

I need to clear the field, smooth the pond. Paper the walls?

(Something in me wants to boil it all down.)

•

Tied to something ancient.

Tie me. (fit to be tied)

•

I have answers but they'll only play out in time.

•

A brutal archaeologist of my own layers:

sandstone, granite, anthracite.

Gold?

•

I gave myself bronchitis as a way of getting closer to my mother?

•

War stories: an organizing principle.

•

I, too, would like to avoid scarring.

•

Talking will kill me? Or not talking?

•

Would this be happening in other languages?

•

One speaks on the exhale; my exhalations are funky and jagged.

•

When my stepfather died, I lost my voice.

When my mother died, I lost my wind.

•

I put all that chocolate in a paper bag and left it at the foot of a tree.

•

a Thanksgiving feast

(no bird)

•

My day—twisted in climax (and anti).

All up and down the light and dark.

•

What kind of therapist will my son be?

Will Freud give him an alibi? (an ally?)

•

These windows are full of tears again.

•

The secret of me was made public;

I'm in the guts of this city now, a real place.

•

Just like music, you paint me beautiful.

•

Time fractures, fragments—often enough to be a pattern.

You'd better believe it.

•

Ever since my mother died, that man, my son, holds out a full cup, offering.

•

Slipped into moans, sighs, syllables. Eventually words, sentences.

•

Sometimes your beauty conflates with the world.

•

A you, addressed, became.

•

My secrets, like pockets turned inside out—

empty!

•

Most things are made on the edge of despair.

•

Loitered so long in Trader Joe's that I thought I was a homeless person.

•

There was a purpose to those excitements.

They got me through. (They got me you.)

She said: The only thing they ever take to an Irish funeral is alcohol.

•

I have been wailing, but almost silently, and to myself.

•

Not sure I have a way to get back from here.

•

I lived.

•

How will I jump between you and not-you?

•

Any audience provides a you. But I will continue exploring.

•

She said: I thought you could take something from here, if you want.

Was that a trick?

•

She feels alive to me today—my mistake.

•

May I focus on your kindness?

(Do you consider that a dodge?)

•

This quiet house—most nearly a mother.

Heat down to 58, I've left the rain coat behind. What if it rains?

Almost gone.

•

She said: Passing gifts over the coffin.

That must be what we've been doing.

•

These many loves kick and jive.

•

I drove past her house.

I kissed the lintel of ours—the closest thing to her coffin.

•

Airport.

Turkish and Arabic—sitting on either side of me!

•

My sister said: You're a choreographed monologue.

No wonder your feet hurt.

•

I will fine-tune my brain, I will settle my body.

•

Allergic to air?

•

Since inhaling things into my lungs and sniffing things into my sinuses, I've begun to taste a place as I walk by.

My taste buds, my eyes? Will I not know your face?

(Will I ingest it each time we meet?)

•

Memory: thick, pliant.

(sometimes unpleasantly stiff)

•

You—a story I tell myself.

•

This soup—spicy but never too salty.

•

Was she giving me her self, her strength, or feeling me (mine), or both?

•

watching my life (a movie)

•

the splattered, half-congealed emotion of airports

•

Not enough time!

•

Endings are also beginnings, of course.

•

We may end on some perfection.

•

There are other nostalgias to visit.

•

Food makes me wheeze.

•

How I feel, returning?

Carry me shoulder-high through this marketplace.

•

Seduced by ends—the possibilities lodged in them.

•

All love stories. Not sure I can write any other kind.

•

Athens, with a view of the Acropolis.

•

My son! I couldn't keep my hands off him!

•

Always sitting on one hotel sofa or another, keyboard on my knees.

•

I need all the self—her and me, both—I can get.

•

In the mirror, I'm getting old!

•

I say to my younger son: When you came out of me, you were so small!

•

Drinking tea, coming to life.

•

So many exclamation points so early in the morning.

Greek didn't even register as a foreign language. Maybe it never does.

•

He ate: mozzarella and prosciutto salad.

Why don't they just call it meat?

•

Livening up?

•

(Frankly, I don't think anyone heard us. This hotel is 3/4 empty, like a gas tank.)

•

Point on the map where all lines meet.

This friendly map—sometimes my only friend.

•

I've seen her twice outside her shop, both times in bookstores.

•

Fourth wall?

Rip, tear! Slash! Burn!

•

Better to think of it as a climax than a termination.

•

I write myself a new body.

•

Breathing is no longer the simple activity it once was, though maybe it was never as simple as I thought.

•

I take every morsel of what you give, turn it about, and out.

•

Sometimes you say: Okay, kid, SCRAM! Outta here! Enough! Take your sticks, your balls, and stones. Your dirty paws and your mud pies. Go find something else to do, another place to be. Come back later but take a break—and give me one, too!

•

The Acropolis on the hill makes me nostalgic;

the light on white buildings makes me crazy with grief.

•

confusing my categories?

•

My sister says: My sister says no to everything!

•

Good and bad objects galore!

•

I'm expert in dividing (hardly conquering, mostly being conquered).

•

Terminate. Terminus. A place the train aims for and ends at. Something like an Auschwitz.

•

We could talk about Sebald, we could talk about Auschwitz. Or Austerlitz. Or Paul Auster. Or the Acropolis in winter light.

•

It's not the specific dream you're after but the fact of one.

•

You throw out a line with bait and never catch more than a glimpse.

But a glimpse that makes you go back for more.

Avid!

•

An insult to pronouns.

(the insult of pronouns?)

•

After a certain point, your parents' sex life becomes liberating.
If they've got one, you can, too!

•

Sun going down—Acropolis in shadow.

•

No greater risk than flying around.

•

Sex: an interpretation of tension.

•

He said: Is that what you told your analyst?

•

The tricks of your trade: Freudian.

•

Last night, the taste of the dessert brought my hands together.
She's clapping, they said, a little astonished.

•

Why do I let my breath get away from me?

•

The architecture of a back: bones.

•

He touched my neck, pressing.
My son's hands are technically acute.

•

Loath to let time pass without marking it, without remarking.

•

I can know what's right for me, I can be my own Discovery Channel.

•

The end sharpens the days.

•

all wound up (until I wind down)

•

Athens! We're staying in a fat hotel! My mother's belly wasn't sunken even when she hadn't eaten for days. Her belly that housed us wasn't gone!

•

Sometimes, spent, I continue twirling.

(no dervish)

•

I thought: Let's make this death a wonderful one.

•

My body often worries me: it worries me, its own shiny glass bead.

•

Dawn.

•

I learned this from you: a fierce holding.

•

What's the difference between a hug and an embrace?

Maybe any touch has its own erotics.

•

Home.

What I realize? All I need is a decent chair.

•

Here, I arrive and pick up my life where I left it, almost.

•

A little over six months ago, I was speaking with my mother from here.

•

No people but him, watching soccer. No reason to talk.

•

Here, the cups may be a little dirty.

Spiders stare at us while we eat.

I believe I will always have something for you.

•

The quiet makes my ears stand up at the sound of his breath.

•

The objects in this house are a little sticky.

•

Either it hasn't hit me that my mother is gone or, being here, where I've always been apart from her, soothes.

•

no hope of touching her ever again

•

A little perplexed, possibly even dismayed that you caught me off-balance.

•

Still charged.

Like my hair!

•

The whirr of the olive-hitters.

•

I return with a smattering of infinities.

•

Pursuing you, I come up short.

Patience and forgetting yield: you come from my heart.

•

Bird. Sheep. Wind. Bell.

The olive pickers have all gone home.

•

This house's dust may tell a story but I'm not sure you'd find it intriguing.

•

The cats unfurl.

Threw away my inhaler.

•

I do whatever I do wherever I am.

Urban, rural, my house, yours.

•

Back to the inestimable satisfaction of cleaning fly shit from windows.

•

I won't know my mother's loss until I've quit you.

•

(I will not lose you.)

•

He brings me to a quiet place, then infuriates me with noisy shoes?

•

If only I could be guaranteed the occasional audience, as with the Patriarch.

(I won't kiss his hand—I would yours.)

•

Wind coming up! Voices carrying!

•

Hands—sometimes too intelligent?

•

A tree throws you back at yourself.

The only thing to want after the death of a mother?

•

I had to have my own small funeral in order to know her death in this place.

He came, too.

•

On the lip of sleep, they come to me.

Last night, he and I were discussing something, cheerfully.

What was he, if not cheerful?

•

Your touch—that squeeze—sometimes gets between me and myself.

I'm sure you have no recollection of that gesture, mine to bear.

•

The strange grey cast to the sky has blown over. Clouds move eastward.

•

I attempt to give you a life—unnecessary.

You're always moving thriftily, craftily, quick-witted and large-hearted.

You bring gesture into relief.

•

I think of stellae: bidding the forever-farewell in stylized gestures.

•

There is so much to do and I still cough.

•

This house is too chipper—self-satisfied.

I can't locate my mother here.

•

At least I can write it.

•

Boiling water for oatmeal.

•

The wind its own (crazy, unpleasant) song.

•

Something like snow!

•

Every time the phone rings in the afternoon, I think it's her.

•

A sliver of window open on the world: male cypress, carob, rock (land) oranged by the dirt (earth), bits of things: green.

•

Tried to meditate—too many flies.

I can't help but swat.

•

Don't want to unmake this self.

•

Ate two shot glasses of olives today: one green, one black.

•

Everything preparation for a final separation.

•

(Sometimes still warm in the certainty of her hold.)

•

Out of wind or just breathless?

•

The truest grief may come at the edge of elation.

•

Sometimes, I eat so well that I'm moved by the fact.

•

The end—an emotionally imagined entity—has entered the scene.

(our hearts)

•

This love isn't only instead-of.

•

Am I fooling myself?

(Only if I think it won't end.)

•

Six-twenty—there's still so much more I want to do today.

•

I can't close this chapter—my heart.

•

In the file called Work, I've got Cooked, Raw, and Simmering.

•

Writing this way (what way?) will always remind me of this self, brought into being opposite you.

Then other selves begin to emerge.

•

I have this plane, a plain before me—

•

But won't I always be able to manufacture at least a semblance of (a) you?

•

Accidental loyalties.

•

But she's been like a mother!

•

When he came in with cupped hands, I said: I hope it's something alive!

But—just an apple.

I asked: Couldn't you have brought me a worm?

•

You said: I thought maybe you had a stash of love letters in your pocket.

I did. I always do.

ACKNOWLEDGMENTS

Maureen: hands
Lizaki and Laura: ears

Jennifer: sister

Constantine: eyes
Alexander: heart

Nick: limbs

Hilary: imagination (generosity)
Rescue Press: prescience (daring)

Thank you to Martha Cooley, Michael Krasny, Louise Steinman, Caitlin Baggott, and Bill Pierce for early readings and comments. Thank you to everyone who attended readings in 2010 and 2011, rendering communal a writer's solitude: a magnificent gift!

Many thanks to the editors of the publications in which the following pieces appeared:

Kenyon Review Online: "Undertaking"
Consequence: "Private"

Very special thanks to Dr. Louis Breger, Askold Melnyczuk, Maggie Nelson, Lia Purpura, Dawn Raffel, Dr. Robert Wallerstein, and Dr. Avivah Gottleib Zornberg for their time and words.

My deepest appreciation to the Rescue Press gang: Zachary Isom, Daniel Khalastchi, Caryl Pagel, Sevy Perez, Alyssa Perry, Hilary Plum, and Zach Savich. What a rescue!

Tommy, your memory is a blessing

Anne Germanacos is the author of the short story collection *In the Time of the Girls* (BOA Editions, 2010). Together with her husband, Nick Germanacos, she ran the Ithaka Cultural Studies Program on the islands of Kalymnos and Crete. She now runs the Germanacos Foundation in San Francisco.

RESCUE
PRESS